The Caretaker's Manual for Forgotten Objects:
A Novel

Brian S. Brijbag, Esq

The Caretaker's Manual for Forgotten Objects: A Novel
© 2025 Brian S. Brijbag, Esq.

First Edition – 2025
ISBN: 979-8-9940221-1-5 (Paperback)
ISBN: 979-8-9940221-0-8 (Hardcover)
ISBN: 979-8-9940221-2-2 (E-Book)

Printed in the United States of America

Legal Notice

Acknowledgment of Artistic Integrity

www.brianbrijbagauthor.com

Dedication

For those who keep the light.

To forget is to return. To remember is to remain.

Light chamber sealed 12 yrs — still humming.

If the Mo Manual writes itself, then who is keeping who?

INSTRUCTIONS FOR DAILY MAINTENANCE OF THE ARCHIVE

1. Dust the objects each morning before light enters the chamber.

2. Catalog any new arrivals in *REGISTRER OF APPARITIONS*. *OF APPARITIONS.*

3. Never throw anything away. *Drawer 314 → cross-reference?*

4. Never ask who they belonged to.

6. If sound or scent is perceived, record but do not respond. *Sound heard again last night — spoon against glass.*

6. Do not look directly at what hums.

7. The Manual will add its own pages as needed. Do not resist this. *Rule 6 added later — who added it)*

Manual feels heavier today. p. 7 appeared overnight.

If it disappears, follow.

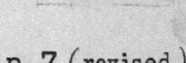

p. 7 (revised)

Table of Contents

Part One – The Archive

Each morning, Emory Vale rose at 5:42 a.m., not because an alarm told him to, but because his body had long since calibrated itself to the rhythm of the sea. Time inside the lighthouse did not pass so much as pool. The clocks had all stopped years ago, or perhaps they'd simply chosen not to argue anymore.

The lighthouse where he lived had long since gone dark. It hadn't warned a ship since the harbor shut down, since the salt had eaten its signal clean off the coast. Now it stood like a monastic pillar, weather-chiseled and mostly forgotten, watching the waves perform their small, relentless theater.

The light chamber had been sealed years ago. Instead, Emory occupied the keeper's quarters two stories down, a narrow suite of stone and shadow. The walls smelled faintly of whale oil and rusted memory. Most mornings, before he made coffee, he sat on the edge of the bed and listened to the wind press questions into the old windowpanes. Then he opened the Manual.

It was not bound like a book. More like a ledger, each page hand-numbered and somewhat warped, as if it had once been submerged. The title was unceremoniously scrawled on the inside cover: The Caretaker's Manual. No author. No date. Just a smudge of blue ink in the lower margin and a faint thumbprint in the corner. Emory didn't know who had left it for him. He had not asked.

The first page was more ritual than instruction.

Dust the objects.
Catalog any new arrivals in the Register of Apparitions.
Never throw anything away.
Never ask who they belonged to.

Emory followed the routine without interpretation. He never questioned why the Register used the word "apparitions" or why the objects arrived at night. He only knew that they did. Always between three and four in the morning. Without sound. Without ceremony. He'd wake to find the door behind the spiral staircase ever so little ajar, the faint smell of cedar and static in the air.

The items varied in size, weight, and presumed consequence. A wooden yo-yo, its string snapped and coiled. A broken wristwatch that ticked intermittently, as though unsure. A child's red shoelace tied in a haphazard knot. A cracked lens from a pair of glasses, its edge worn soft. Emory collected each one carefully with cotton gloves, as instructed, and placed them into labeled drawers inside the Archive Room. Every drawer had a date. Some had only a word. Some had none at all.

He did not believe the objects were lost. Not in the conventional sense. They had been dislodged, perhaps, from the dense tangle of memory and routine, from drawers never opened and bags never unpacked. They had not been misplaced. They had been forgotten.

And forgetting, Emory had come to believe, was not absence. It was relocation. A kind of quiet exile. His job was to notice what the world had tried to abandon.

There was comfort in this, in the tactile precision of tending to the lost. It asked nothing of him beyond attention. The Manual never praised, never warned. It offered only the steps, the sequence, the ritual.

And for a man who no longer trusted the fluency of his own speech, ritual was the last language he could speak without error. But even the most practiced rituals eventually falter. One morning, something slipped in sideways, quiet as breath.

A sound, faint and familiar, rose where silence had stood.

Not the arrival of an object - those slipped in unheard, as always - but the memory of a sound stirred by touch. Emory had lifted a porcelain doorknob from the Archive Room's floor, its edges cool and smoothed with use. As he turned it in his palm, a small noise bloomed in the back of his mind: the delicate clink of a spoon against glass. Not a real sound. Not something in the room. But clear, specific, with that peculiar fidelity memory reserves for the trivial.

He stood still for several minutes, the object balanced in his hand, waiting for the sensation to pass or sharpen. It did neither. Instead, it nested itself somewhere behind the eyes. A clink, a spoon, a glass. Nothing more. But it did not feel random.

Two days later, the same thing happened again.

This time with a plastic pencil sharpener, its blade long rusted, the casing opaque with age. When he rotated it, testing its weight, the room seemed to fill - just faintly - with the acrid sweetness of burnt sugar. Not fire. Not danger. A smell more domestic than threatening, like a stovetop mistake made by someone learning to love themselves again. Emory dropped the sharpener, not from fear but reverence. He bent to retrieve it slowly, as one might handle an old photograph found beneath a floorboard.

By the end of the week, a pattern had formed.

Not every object triggered a sensation. But those that did carried something precise: the static flicker of a television half-muted in another room. The dry snap of onion skin paper turning in a hymnal. The warmth of laundry just removed from the dryer - though he had not owned one in decades.

These were not memories he could place. Not as his own. Yet they resonated with the muted intimacy of something once held and long since set down.

Lately the objects were no longer content to suggest. They had begun to remember for him.

He began keeping track.

At first, he tried writing the sensations into the Register, but the format resisted them. Too clinical, too narrow. So instead, he cleared a space on the west wall of the Archive Room - an expanse of stone once used to hang storm gear - and constructed what he called the Memory Chart. There were no headings. No legend. Just a grid of butcher paper and thumbtacks, each square marked with the date of an object's arrival and the sensory trace it produced.

"12 May – sour breath / velvet seatback"
"15 May – skin salt / cassette rewinding"
"18 May – voice, male, almost singing"

The Chart grew unevenly, like moss, favoring some weeks over others. Occasionally, an object would arrive that seemed to resonate with a previous one, as if they had once coexisted in the same drawer or moment, parted now but not severed.

The lighthouse had grown quieter in response. Not empty, but attenuated, as though the very air understood something was being drawn into the open. Not confessed - Emory would not use that word - but exposed, carefully, without judgment.

And still the Manual said nothing about sensation. Nothing about smells or sounds or the sudden ache behind the sternum when touching a faded bus ticket from 1989.

But Emory kept cataloguing. He began waking earlier. Sometimes he'd drift back to sleep with a catalogued scent still lingering at the base of his throat, like the aftertaste of someone else's memory.

He did not know what he was uncovering, only that the Chart felt less like a record of arrivals and more like the negative space of something being assembled.

Not a pattern.
Not yet.
But the outline of a language he had once known how to speak.

And perhaps, somewhere within it, a sentence with his name.

The next object arrived quietly, almost embarrassed to be counted among the rest.

A paperclip. Not silver, but coppered, dulled at the bend and warped, as if it had once been forced to hold too many pages. It arrived alone, coiled like an afterthought on the Archive Room floor, beside the brass drawer labeled Unclassified – Spring Arrivals. Emory almost overlooked it. It looked too ordinary, like something dropped from a pocket or swept in by accident.

He picked it up anyway, careful not to straighten its curve.

As he turned it between his fingers, something in his chest shifted - subtly, as if a button had been pressed behind his ribs. He was no longer in the Archive Room, not exactly. The temperature changed. The air thinned. And without warning or grandeur, a scene rose into view - not in front of him, but inside him, behind his eyelids, uninvited but unmistakable.

A girl sat cross-legged on a patchy carpet, holding a yellow folder in her lap. The walls around her were covered in posters: planets, cartoon owls, a crude phonics chart with the letter Q peeling off. The girl was maybe eight. She had a stubborn part in her hair, too deep on one side, and she was humming something tuneless under her breath. The copper paperclip held her worksheet together, a coloring exercise half-filled with shaky blue crayon. She smiled without looking up.

Emory knew this room.

It had been a resource classroom. Lincoln Elementary. His daughter's second-grade teacher had asked for help sorting reading levels one afternoon, and Emory - newly retired then, eager to be useful - had said yes. He hadn't planned to stay long. He was uncomfortable around children not his own. But his daughter had smiled when he agreed, and he had wanted to be the kind of man who said yes to small things.

He had sat at a kidney-shaped table near the girl, his hands too large for the delicate paper stacks, trying not to disturb the order. The girl had dropped her pencil. He had bent to retrieve it.

And when their eyes met, just for a moment, she had asked him if he was someone's dad or someone's grandpa. He had laughed but couldn't remember now what he'd said.

He had forgotten this memory. Not neglected. Not discarded. Forgotten, in the purest sense. As though it had never happened. And yet now, standing in the Archive Room, the air still carried the chalk-dust stillness of that classroom. The clip felt warm. His fingertips tingled.

He placed the object on the desk beside the Memory Chart and wrote in smaller handwriting than usual.

"23 May – yellow folder / blue crayon / quiet hum / someone's dad or someone's grandpa"

The phrase sat awkwardly in the margin, too personal to be neutral, too real to erase. He stared at it longer than he needed to. Then, gently, he slipped the paperclip into a new drawer. One he labeled not by date or sensation, but with a name.

Etta.

The name didn't appear in the Manual. He didn't expect it to. The Manual had no section for naming. Naming made things particular. And particulars were harder to forget.

That night, sleep did not come easily. The waves seemed louder than usual. Or maybe closer. Emory lay still beneath a wool blanket and thought about the question that girl had asked in the classroom. It hadn't meant anything then. But now, in the hush of the lighthouse, it echoed louder than it should have.

Was he someone's dad
or someone's grandpa
or someone left between the two?

In the dark, he reached out toward the Manual on the nightstand. He didn't open it. He just let his fingers rest there, as if to reassure the book - and himself - that the rituals still held.

But the paperclip had shifted something. Not much. Just enough to remind him that even those who tend the forgotten are not immune to being remembered.

And that memory, when it comes, does not ask permission.

The paperclip became a pivot. Not in the drawer, but in his hands, in his mind. A small hinge on something larger.

After its arrival, Emory found it harder to move through his routines with the same silent certainty. The objects still came, still nested themselves in corners or curled up like sleeping animals beneath the window ledge, but now he hesitated before labeling them. His pen would hover above the Register longer than usual. The descriptors came slower. Sometimes, not at all.

There was a small plastic keychain that looked like it had once held a grocery rewards tag. No more than a sliver of faded blue plastic, its barcode long rubbed smooth. When he touched it, Emory felt a sharpness behind the eyes - not pain exactly, but a sensation like squinting into memory. He was standing in a fluorescent-lit aisle, surrounded by the hum of refrigeration units. Someone was laughing. A woman. But the sound was hollow, warped at the edges like a cassette played too many times.

He tried to place the laugh. It sounded familiar in the way that dreams do - plausible, vivid, and utterly unrooted. He wrote in the margin of the Memory Chart: "Plastic tag – aisle 6? / woman laughing / not my wife? maybe my wife?"

It unsettled him. Not because he couldn't remember, but because he almost did. There was something cruel in proximity. The feeling of truth just out of reach, like a name on the tip of the tongue that never arrives.

Other objects began doing the same. They no longer returned full recollections, but fragments in conflict with one another.

A blue ink pen yielded the scent of lavender soap and the vision of a checkbook that did not match his own handwriting.

A baby's sock evoked a car seat in the back of a hatchback he had never driven.

A man's leather glove brought with it a feeling of shame so vivid he had to sit down, though he could not name its source.

The Chart grew more erratic. He abandoned the grid structure and began using thread to connect entries - red for sensation, blue for image, yellow for emotion. The wall began to resemble a crime board from a detective show, though no crime had occurred. At least, none he could remember.

He stopped using the Manual for a time.

It sat on the desk, spine softening, the pages curling faintly at the corners as though aware of their neglect. Emory found himself resenting it - its false assurance, its bland certainties. Dust the objects. Catalog the arrivals. Never ask who they belonged to.

But the objects were asking for him now.

Sometimes he would wake with the taste of a memory in his mouth, bitter and metallic, and rise to find nothing new in the

Archive Room. No object. No scent. Just a hollow feeling, like something had tried to visit but found him absent.

He began leaving notes for himself, handwritten and tucked into the pockets of his cardigan or slipped beneath the tea tin in the kitchen.

"You are Emory Vale."
"This is the lighthouse."
"The ocean is real."
"You had a daughter."
"Your wife left. Or died. Or both."

One morning he found a note he didn't remember writing. The handwriting matched his own, but the phrasing was not something he would have used.

"You were loved once. That should be enough."

He didn't know whether it was a comfort or a rebuke.

The lighthouse, for its part, remained unchanged. The beams of morning rays still angled through the small stained-glass window on the eastern wall, casting puddles of color across the floorboards. The wind still pressed gently at the stone like a child testing the patience of an old door.

But inside Emory, something had begun to loosen.

A quiet untying.
A slow fall inward.
Not into madness.
Into memory.

And memory, he was beginning to learn, was neither fixed nor faithful. It was a smoke, and he had mistaken it for stone.

What's next arrived with no scent, no sound, no accompanying flicker of memory. Only weight. And the suggestion that it had always been there.

The brass key simply was.

Emory found it just before dawn, resting atop the threshold of the Archive Room door as though it had been placed there deliberately. It hadn't skittered into a corner like the others, hadn't nestled into fabric or waited in the crook of a stair. It sat upright, gleaming faintly in the low glow, entirely unhidden.

Its surface was warm. Not ambient-warm, not touched-by-sunlight warm. Warm the way a hand is. Alive. Emory held it for a long time without moving. The metal was smooth but imperfect - worn in a way that suggested use and use over time. The shaft was short, the teeth few. Just three notches, sharp and clean. On its bow, barely legible beneath a layer of tarnish, was a single number:

314

He turned it over. No engraving. No logo. Just the number. A room number, perhaps. A code. A floor. A year.

314 meant nothing to him. But his body disagreed.

He felt it in the thorax first, a compression, like a breath caught mid-way and held without cause. Then a subtle tremor at the base of the neck. The same sensation he'd once had as a child on the verge of being scolded for something he could not remember doing.

He brought the key to the desk and set it beside the Memory Chart. It murmured faintly, almost imperceptibly, as if responding to proximity. He watched it for a full hour, waiting for sensation, for a flash, for some signal.

Nothing came. No scent, no sound. Only heat.

He tried to catalog it, as he had with every other item.

Date: 2 June
Item: brass key
Sensation: None

Notes: Number 314. Weight $\approx$ 20g. Emits low-grade warmth. No emotional or sensory recall.

Then, after a long pause, he added:

Possibly mine.

It was the first time he'd ever written that.

He tried to dismiss the idea, to assign the key to a broader mythology, to file it away in the collective debris of memory that didn't belong to him. But the key resisted abstraction. It felt particular.

For hours, he stared at the number. 314. It gnawed at the edges of thought. A locker combination? An address? A date? No memory rose to meet it, but the pressure behind his eyes mounted until he had to dim the lamps and rest.

When he dreamt, he was walking down a hallway. That much he remembered upon waking. Fluorescent lights hummed above. Vinyl floor tiles stretched in both directions. Every door had a number. Some he passed without notice. Others he counted.

310.
311.
312.
313.

He woke before the next.

The room was cold. The key was no longer on the desk.

For a brief, irrational moment, he wondered if he'd dreamt it. But when he rose and stepped barefoot into the Archive Room, there it was - on the floor beneath the Memory Chart, teeth down, almost buried beneath a constellation of thread and notes.

It had moved.

Or been moved.

He picked it up again. Still warm. Now almost hot.

There were no doors in the lighthouse with numbered locks. No drawers. No trunks. He opened every compartment anyway, paced the stairs twice, checked behind the lantern housing, beneath the floorboards in the kitchen. Nothing yielded. No slot matched. No mechanism called for a key.

That night, he sat in the center of the Archive Room, key in one hand, Manual in the other.

He flipped to the final page, which had always been blank.

Now, it was not.

In faint, looping script, a new entry had appeared:

"If it flutters, it belongs to you. If it disappears, follow."

Emory stared at the words for a long time, his hand trembling around the metal. He whispered the sentence aloud, though the voice that came out didn't quite sound like his own.

Then he closed the Manual and waited for the key to vanish.

And when it did, it left no mark. Just a faint indentation on his palm. And the certainty that something had unlocked.

Not out there.

Within.

For three days, Emory did not search.

He continued his rituals - dusting, cataloging, filing - but he did them with less conviction, as though participating in a liturgy whose meaning had expired. The Archive Room felt altered. Not changed, exactly, but heavier, like it knew something he did not.

The key had disappeared as the Manual said it would, but the warmth remained in his palm for hours afterward. Even now, when he flexed his fingers, he could feel the phantom of its shape - a presence without pressure, a memory without mass.

He did not speak the number aloud again. He feared giving it too much reality, feared shaping the thing into a destination when it might instead be a warning. Or a confession.

At night, his dreams thickened.

He saw doors. Hundreds of them. All closed. Some warped with age, others so new the paint still shone. They lined endless corridors with no architecture - just blank space, like a blueprint sketched into darkness. When he tried to open them, his hands held nothing.

In one dream, he saw a child's hand reach for the knob ahead of him. Not his daughter's. Not any child he could name. Just the small, certain hand of someone unafraid. The door swung inward, and Emory stepped toward it - but woke before passing through.

Each morning, he sat longer on the edge of the bed. The light that once filtered through the stained-glass pane now looked different to him. Not dimmer. Not brighter. Just other. It painted the floorboards in strange geometries. He began to think it was not light at all, but some form of memory refracted.

He stopped adding to the Memory Chart. The wall remained, thread and pins and notes all intact, but Emory no longer felt tethered to it. The Chart had once been a record. Now it felt like a decoy. An act of curation to distract from what was being buried deeper.

He began to wonder if he had ever really forgotten anything.

Perhaps the forgetting had only ever been a kindness. A deferral. A hallway he passed without looking through the door. The key, then, was not a gift. Not even a tool. It was a question made solid. A key is not an answer. It is the implication of a lock.

And a lock implies something was meant to be kept from you.

Or within you.

Emory no longer trusted the Manual. Its rules had once brought order, but order, he realized, was simply a slower kind of fear. The objects had never needed dusting. The Archive did not care for his taxonomy. He had not been tending it.

It had been tending him.

And what now? Was he being prepared for something?
Or unmade in slow, deliberate increments?

He wrote nothing down that day. Not in the Register. Not on the wall. He simply stood in the doorway of the Archive Room and stared at the space where the key had once sat. The threshold. A word he now understood differently.

Thresholds are not meant to be admired. They are meant to be crossed.

Still, he did not move.

He wasn't ready.
Or perhaps, readiness had never been the point.

He was no longer asking where the key had gone. He was beginning to ask who had turned it last.

And what it had once locked away.

He didn't remember learning it - only knowing it, gradually, like light revealing the shape of something long motionless.

It did not arrive all at once.

There was no grand unveiling, no sudden crack of comprehension. The realization came in increments - hesitations, remnants of sounds, the subtle way the Archive Room began to feel less like a place he worked in and more like a place that had always been inside him.

It began with the mitten.

He had cataloged it early in his time at the lighthouse. A child's wool mitten, green with a white stripe near the cuff, the yarn partially unraveled at the thumb. He had noted its size, the faint smell of crayon wax, the soft pilling that suggested long use. At the time, it had stirred nothing. A forgotten winter thing. Commonplace. Comforting.

But now, weeks later, a memory surfaced - not as an image, but as a sound: the reverberation of a store intercom calling for assistance in aisle three. The rustle of plastic bags. A voice - his voice - rising in sharpness as he called a name he hadn't spoken aloud in years.

Etta Vale.

I am someone's dad.

He remembered the mitten in her hand that Tuesday. How she'd tugged it off absentmindedly while reaching for a bag of animal crackers. How he had told her - just a moment, stay close - and how, when he turned back, she was gone. Only for minutes. Maybe less. But the cold terror that bloomed in those minutes had scorched something permanent into him. She was found, unharmed, crouched near a display of oranges.

But the mitten was never recovered. Until now.

He sat with it for a long time, turning it slowly, the threads catching in the ridges of his fingertips. It was hers. Not similar. Not reminiscent. Hers.

He almost set it back down - almost just placed it quietly beside the others, as if it had never arrived. As if it were just another woolen artifact from someone else's winter. A forgivable confusion. A trick of scent and shape.

Some things dissolved when he released them. Others entered him. Each behaved according to what forgetting required.

He told himself it might not be the same one. That there were surely thousands like it. That memory, once softened, could be made to fit anything.

But the lie wouldn't hold.

So he kept holding it. And cataloged it.

The lens came next.

It had arrived cracked, a map of delicate ruin at one edge. He had cataloged it, assigned no owner, assumed it belonged to no one in particular. But now, without effort, he remembered the way his wife's glasses had struck the linoleum that final night. The argument had been quiet. Not dramatic. Just a slow erosion, like rust eating through the hull of a boat. She had packed quickly. One suitcase. One glance back. The glasses had fallen from her coat pocket as she turned to go. He had picked them up, placed them on the table, and never spoken of them again.

He had not followed her. He had not called. The lens in the Archive Room bore the same crack. Even the same faint smudge at the corner, like a fingerprint blurred by indecision.

Then came the key.

He had almost convinced himself it was metaphor. A symbol. An artifact from someone else's story. But the dreams had returned - fluorescent lights, numbered doors, the antiseptic quiet of a hospital corridor. Room 314. The room where his mother had died. He now knew.

He had received the call late, long after visiting hours. They told him she'd been asking for him. That she had asked repeatedly.

He had not gone.

He told himself he wouldn't have made it in time. That it wouldn't have changed anything. But the truth was simpler, and colder.

He couldn't bear the weight of being seen again - not by someone whose memory of him remained whole.

The key. It had returned not as symbol ... not as prophecy.

But as proof.

He stood before the Memory Chart and began peeling the entries from the wall. Not all of them. Just enough. One by one, he lifted them, held them to the light, and saw what he had missed. Each note, each thread, each object - it wasn't a map of loss.

It was a ledger of release.

These were not the world's forgotten things.

They were his.

Everything he had abandoned. Or misplaced. Or failed to carry.

He stepped back and took in the Archive Room anew.

This was not a collection site. It was not a repository of communal forgetting.

It was Emory.

Every shelf. Every drawer. Every whispered hum that came when he opened a box. The room was not haunted. It was inhabited.

And the Manual, for all its precision, had never said that. Because the Manual had been written for someone else. A prior caretaker. A different archivist. Someone who stood outside the room.

But Emory was not outside.

He was the collection.

He was the forgetting.

He was the thing being kept.

And the key was gone.

Once, the lighthouse had turned. He remembered that now - not vividly, but in fragments: the slow mechanical groan as the beam swept the horizon, the brief glint on distant hulls as ships blinked back, the white slash of light cutting through fog thick enough to swallow names. It had been a warning. A guide. A promise that someone was watching the edge. But even then, there had been nights when the beam failed to catch what mattered. A boat too close. A signal too late. He wondered if the light had ever saved anyone - or if, like him, it had only ever been trying to.

He lasted three more days.

Three days of ritual performed in silence, of object arrivals met with neither pen nor memory. The Archive Room had grown too dense with itself. He could feel the air thickening, not with dust or humidity, but with some unnamed tension, as if the room knew he was circling a door he had not yet dared to open.

The drawer had always been there. High on the east wall, just beneath the broken clock that hadn't moved in years. It was smaller than the others, shallow and square, the wood darker, more warped. A heavy brass latch sealed it shut - not locked, just fastened, as though daring rather than preventing.

Its label was handwritten in a different script than the rest.

"DO NOT OPEN - REGISTERED BUT UNFILED"

He had never touched it. Not once. It was the single rule he obeyed without interpretation. There had always been a feeling about that drawer - one he couldn't name, like the fear that arises when a child first senses that silence can be wrong.

But now, with the key gone, the Chart stripped, and the weight of recognition sinking deeper into his bones, Emory no longer felt beholden to the Manual. The book remained closed on the desk. He had stopped turning its pages. It had served its purpose, or maybe it had never served him at all.

He stood before the drawer at dusk.

The light slanted sharply through the stained glass, turning the far wall the color of blood oranges. He hesitated, fingertips hovering over the latch. His breath caught, not from fear, but from a sense that something irreversible was about to begin - not an action, but a letting go.

He released the clasp.

The drawer opened with a reluctant creak, the wood sighing like it hadn't been disturbed in decades.

Inside was only one object.

A small cassette recorder. Plastic, grey, its surface dulled by time and touch. Unremarkable in shape but softened by use, as if it had outlasted its own purpose. The buttons were worn, their letters faded by touch. It bore no label. No cassette. Just the machine itself.

But when Emory pressed play, the spools began to turn.

There was a brief crackle of static. Then a pause. Then a voice.

Not his own.

A child's voice.

Not a recording of conversation. No background noise. Just a single sentence, spoken with careful intention, as if read aloud from memory or prayer.

"You can stop now. It's okay to forget some things."

The voice was familiar in a way that defied language. Not recognition by sound, but by consequence. Emory felt it in his torso first, that same compression he'd known when holding the brass key. Then lower, in his stomach, in the old ache that used to come just before sleep, when his mind would flinch at the idea that something important had been misplaced forever.

The child's voice had no inflection. No emotional tug. Just clarity. Permission.

The tape clicked to a stop.

Emory stood frozen, the recorder still in his hand. The air in the Archive Room changed. Not temperature. Not scent.
Just weight. As if something had been lifted that he didn't realize he'd been carrying.

He replayed the tape. Once. Twice. No change. No elaboration. Just the same sentence, each time spoken in that neutral, patient tone.

"You can stop now. It's okay to forget some things."

He did not cry. That would have been too easy. Too cinematic. Instead, he sat on the wooden stool at the center of the room and listened to the tape one final time, eyes closed, body still, as the sun bled into the sea outside.

What broke him was not the voice itself, but the way the sentence landed.

Not as an answer.

As a release.

He thought about the Archive Room, about every labeled drawer, every clipped tag, every thread on the wall. It had all been an effort to hold on - to organize what had refused to stay.

But the voice hadn't asked him to remember.

It had blessed the forgetting.

And in that moment, Emory understood.

This had never been a lighthouse. Not in the traditional sense. It had not warned others. It had not guided ships.

It had held him. A place not to see out from, but to dissipate inside.

He reached for his coat.

It hung, as always, on the hook beside the door, stiff with salt air and lined with old wool. He hadn't worn it in weeks. As he slid his hand into the pocket, his fingers met something unexpected - small, cool, and perfectly round.

He drew it out without ceremony.

A marble.

Clear glass, with a thread of green coiled inside like a trapped breath. He turned it slowly between his thumb and forefinger, holding it up to the window. The morning light caught in its center and held.

He didn't remember putting it there. Didn't remember owning it. It didn't call up a face or a place or a voice.

But it fit in his hand.

Perfectly.

He didn't catalogue it. Didn't name it. He simply slipped it back into his pocket, where it made no sound at all. He sat, and the old chair accepted him. Outside, the sea leaned in close and spoke the day's last secrets to the stone.

He woke before the light.

No dreams. Or perhaps only the kind too soft to leave footprints. The air in the quarters felt thinner than usual, hollowed by something that had finished happening in the night. Emory rose without ceremony, dressed without thought. The Manual lay closed on the table, undisturbed. He did not bring it with him.

He stepped into the morning with the key now again in his palm. He didn't remember finding it - only waking to it, warm in his hand, as if it had been waiting all along.

It no longer throbbed. The warmth had gone. It felt like any other object now - dull, metallic, inert. And yet, the weight of it had changed. Or he had.

The cliff path behind the lighthouse curved narrowly, clinging to the rock face like something uncertain of its own right to exist. He had walked it before, but never in full. Not to the end. Not past the old fog bell or the moss-darkened fence. Not to where the land forgot itself and gave way to cliff and salt and sea.

But today he continued.

He did not rush. His gait was measured, like someone accompanying a process rather than enacting one. The wind tugged at his sleeves. The gulls overhead cried in language too old to be translated. Still, he walked.

Near the base of the lighthouse's northern wall, half-concealed behind a curtain of thorned ivy, he found it.

A door.

Low, narrow, metal long surrendered to rust. Not something built for passage, but for hiding. It bore no knob. Only a keyhole - round, deliberate, exactly the shape of the silence Emory had been carrying for years.

He hesitated. Not from fear. From familiarity.

He had never seen the door before, but his hand moved to it without question. As if rehearsed.

The key fit. Smoothly. Not a catch, not a grind. It turned with the soft finality of a sentence reaching its period.

The door opened inward.

No stairs. No ladder. No archive. Just a narrow recess carved into the rock - empty, clean, dustless. A frame, nothing more. Beyond it, the sea extended toward a soft gray horizon, its rhythm patient and unconcerned.

Emory stood in the threshold.

He did not enter. He did not retreat.

He simply looked.

There was no sound but the tide breathing against rocks.

After a while, he sat. The stone was cold. He did not mind.

He opened his hand and let the key fall. It didn't clatter. It didn't strike the bone of the earth.

It vanished. Not with magic. Not with spectacle. Simply gone.

Emory sat still for a long time, unsure whether anything had changed. The sea continued. The sky did not clarify. Behind him, the lighthouse loomed in silence.

He did not look back.

But his body leaned modestly forward, as if listening for something just beyond the wind.

He closed his eyes, exhaled once, and listened - not for instruction, not for memory, not even for meaning.

Just listened.

And somewhere, deep in the place where forgetting touches forgiveness, something loosened.

Or waited.

Or called forward.

Part Two – The Threshold

Emory did not so much step through the door as lose the distinction between where stepping ended and entering began.

The air caught him. Not with resistance, but with understanding - an almost imperceptible gesture of acceptance, as though the space beyond the rusted frame had been expecting him.

The shift was immediate, but not violent. The world did not tilt or darken. It simply unstitched.

The cliffside air, the ache of stone beneath his boots, the soft percussion of surf below - all folded backward into silence, as if someone had closed a book in mid-sentence. The silence that followed was not absence. It was substance. It pressed gently against him, tactile and whole, a silence so dense it had weight.

He waited for his eyes to adjust, for the world to arrange itself into something nameable. It didn't.

There was no sea.
No sky.
No horizon to divide one from the other.

He stood inside a colorless expanse that shimmered faintly, as though the air had been polished. The light had no origin but arrived everywhere at once, ambient and patient, the way dawn might appear if it forgot to finish happening. Everything here existed in the tense between what had been and what had not yet begun.

When he turned, expecting at least the outline of the lighthouse, he saw only a column of vapor, pale and trembling, like breath rising from the mouth of something enormous. It flickered faintly, once, twice, then stilled. The shape of the tower lingered within it - an afterimage more felt than seen - before dissolving completely.

The act of watching it disappear hurt more than he expected. Not grief exactly, but a disorientation, the way one feels when a word long used suddenly reveals itself as foreign.

He closed his eyes. The darkness there was more stable. Inside it, he heard something - not sound, but the idea of it - the hum of machinery that had never existed here: the slow grind of the lighthouse lens, the faint rhythm of waves beneath stone.

If it disappears, follow.

The sentence rose unbidden, not as recollection but as beam. It vibrated low in his sternum, less command than continuation. He placed his palm flat against his breastbone and felt the thud there syncing to something larger, something that did not belong to time.

He opened his eyes again.

The world - or whatever stood in for it - had acquired a suggestion of ground. Not solid, exactly, but cooperative. His shoes met resistance, faint as breath on glass. When he shifted his weight, the room's reply came first - the soft report of his step preceding the movement that caused it.

He froze.
Then tried again.

Once more, the sound came before action: the future remembering him before he arrived. The realization unsettled him, yet it made a quiet kind of sense. In memory, all things occur out of order. Perhaps, he thought, this place was built from that logic - the call before the event, the consequence that dreams its own cause.

Understanding didn't matter anymore. The knowing could arrive later, or never.

He began to walk.

Each step produced two impressions: one that belonged to the body, and one that belonged to the place. The latter arrived first, a faint indentation of light that formed beneath his feet and held its shape even after he moved on. When he looked back, he saw not footprints but small pools of luminescence, as though the act of walking had awakened something beneath the surface.

The air smelled of warm salt and old paper. The scent startled him with its familiarity - the very fragrance of the Archive, only inverted, as though turned inside out by the act of crossing. He drew it in slowly. It was comforting and wrong at once, like a childhood room glimpsed years later: smaller, quieter, haunted by absence that did not hurt until named.

He whispered to the air without meaning to. The words came out like exhalations. "Where are you?" he asked, though he did not know to whom the question was addressed.

The remembered sound returned before the voice had finished leaving him.
Where are you ... where are you ...
Each repetition thinner, less obedient to his tone, until the final iteration sounded almost compassionate.

He continued walking.

Distance here was an act of faith. The landscape - or lack of it - shifted not because he moved, but because he decided he had. Shapes began to assemble themselves from the periphery of his focus: faint architectures of vapor, half-remembered outlines. A chair. A clock face. The hint of a staircase ascending into nowhere. They appeared only when not looked at directly, as if attention embarrassed them back into invisibility.

The sound of his own breathing seemed layered, delayed, as though another breath - older, slower - was trying to synchronize with it.

He stopped. The stillness had gravity.

When he lifted his hand before him, his fingers blurred at the edges, transparent but not absent. They wavered, their outlines rippling as though submerged. He flexed them, watching as they took longer than they should to obey. It was not decay, he realized. It was negotiation. The body was renegotiating its shape.

A glow of warmth gathered in his chest again. It spread outward, threading along veins like soft light beneath skin. Each beat carried memory: not images, not events, but textures - wool against his wrist, the ridged surface of a key, the delicate friction of paper under thumb. The physical ghosts of what he had once handled. The things he had kept alive by naming.

He thought of the Manual - of its rigid script and unblinking certainty - and realized that no instruction had ever truly prepared him for this. There was no entry for crossing, no ritual for unmaking. The Manual's silence on this threshold was not omission; it was reverence.

The mist ahead thickened, then broke open like fabric torn by a gentle hand. Through it, a pale expanse emerged - neither sky nor ground, but something between. It shimmered faintly, not with light but with recollection. Within it moved shadows, slow and aimless, as though caught in the act of remembering themselves.

He felt them before he saw them - tremors in the air, soft as breeze through reeds. They passed through him without friction, each one leaving behind a faint impression: the smell of bread cooling, a chord on a piano, the whisper of a name that almost belonged to him.

He whispered back. Not words. Just breath. The exchange felt holy.

Behind him, the remembrance of the lighthouse flickered one last time - a dim silhouette suspended in fog - and then went out. The act of its vanishing did not feel like loss. It felt like punctuation.

Emory exhaled and took another step.

The ground shifted underfoot, acquiring texture. Not stone, not sand - something finer, something living. It flexed gently with his weight, like the surface of deep water pretending to be earth.

He thought of the sea again. Of how, in certain weather, the horizon disappears and one cannot tell where the water ends and the air begins. This place felt like that moment, eternalized. A place where the world had forgotten which side of itself it belonged to.

He tried to mark the air with his hand, to test whether it would remember the movement. The gesture lingered, drawn in light, then folded back into nothing.

He began to understand. This was not a new world. This was the inside of remembering - the architecture of his own mind, rendered spatial and strange. Everything that had ever existed in the pause between thought and recollection had gathered here, waiting.

He reached instinctively for the pocket where the marble had once been. His fingers found only emptiness, but the warmth remained, embedded in the lining. He wondered if it, too, had crossed over, or if it had simply become him.

He looked down again. The luminous footprints behind him had begun to fade. The first step - the one closest to the door -

was already gone. The next dimmed as he watched, until only a faint shimmer remained. It occurred to him that the world was unmaking his path even as he walked it. No return. No retracing. Only forward, into a place where forward might not mean direction.

He did not resist.

The tremble in his upper body steadied, then slowed, matching some unseen rhythm. It was not his heart he was hearing now - it was the rising. The sea he had left behind still lived inside him, and here it remembered its original form: not water, but memory.

He closed his eyes and let the rhythm guide him.

The scent of salt and paper deepened, layered now with something else - iron, smoke, the faint sweetness of cedar. The sensory palette of his life rearranging itself into hymn.

He thought of the objects one by one. The paperclip. The mitten. The lens. The key. Each one flickered behind his eyelids like constellations momentarily brightening before final eclipse. They had led him here, every small relic conspiring toward this crossing.

He whispered their names into the air. Each vanished upon saying, but the silence that followed felt grateful.

The light around him began to oscillate faintly, synchronizing to his heartbeat, and for a moment he could see the faint outline of his own shadow cast ahead - thin, translucent, trembling like the reflection of a bird across shallow water.

Then, in one smooth motion, the horizon folded forward. The air seemed to inhale. And Emory was carried - gently, without impact - through the last layer of separation.

He did not fall.
He did not ascend.

He entered.

The transition was neither death nor birth. It was continuity -
the quiet conversion of matter into memory.

The air beyond accepted him wholly, enfolding him like paper
into an old book, and in that embrace he understood: the
threshold had never been a line to cross but a veil to recognize.
The boundary between the material and the mnemonic had not
merged. It had merely reminded him that they were never
separate.

As he disappeared into the pale expanse, the last reply of his
voice lingered in the air, not as a plea or question but as
acknowledgment -
a whisper shaped like revival and gratitude:

I am still here.

The words did not travel far. They didn't need to.

Somewhere behind him, far back where the sea still believed in
gravity and time, a faint sound answered -
the slow, deliberate turning of a lighthouse lens,
once more finding its rhythm.

He moved toward what announced itself as a shoreline only
after he had already believed it was one. At first there was
merely a soft inhalation along the colorless field, a faint
corrugation of light the way wind ribs the skin of shallow
water. Then the suggestion thickened into distance. The
distance became approach. And what had been a bright blank
began to quiver in bands, pale upon paler, until motion
revealed itself as the sea's pull.

Only the unmooring was wrong.

The waves did not come from the reachless horizon,
shouldering forward, then falling back into themselves. They
assembled inland and rolled toward him, into the land, as
though the continent were a lung exhaling the sea. The crests

curled soundlessly, pushed by no wind he could feel, and slid
past his boots like silk, leaving the ground wetter behind
them than before. It was the gesture of retreat performed in the
wrong direction - rivers remembering their source and deciding
to return there.

He stood still and let the first of those inward waves travel
through him. It met his shins with no cold, no sting, only the
damp impression of having been touched by a memory. When
it thinned around his ankles, he looked down and saw that his
footprints - those faint pools of light his steps had pressed into
the surface - did not wash away. They brightened. Each inward
flux of water fed them, as if the sea were lighting his path
instead of erasing it.

The next swell reached higher, a pale belt across his knees, and
with it something moved in the water - dark, coin-sized, then
gone. He bent as the line passed, palm open to the receding
brightness, and felt the light cling to him, not sticky, not
electric - obedient. The afterglow bled onto his skin, and for an
instant his hand looked like a map of shallow constellations.

He did not speak. Words here made replies out of order, and
silence kept its shape better.

Another wave formed itself behind him, gathering where the
blankness used to be. It rolled forward with patient conviction,
and now there were things caught in its glass. Not shapes
pretending at furniture or doorways, not the silhouettes that
embarrassed themselves when looked at too directly -
but objects, rendered with the stubborn particularity of the held
and the lost.

A wooden yo-yo, its string snapped and furred with use,
bobbed in the incoming face of water. Beside it, a green wool
mitten rode the wave knuckle-first, as if a child's hand might
still be inside. The worn bow of a brass key turned slowly,
teeth catching light. There was a grocery tag, a cracked lens, a
red shoelace tied into a knot that could not decide whether it
wanted to be a bow. Each item drifted as if the slow reclaim

had learned the grammar of his Archive and was repeating it
back to him, fluent and calm.

They were only ever half-visible. The water's body disclosed
them, then revised its mind, and they went obscure again. But
whenever one drifted within his reach, the world seemed to
pause - an intake of breath long enough for him to decide
whether to touch.

He did.

He reached where the yo-yo troubled the water, and the instant
his finger made contact, the yo-yo vanished, not dissolving
but departing - as though it had simply remembered where it
needed to be. In its place came the soft lift of a child's laugh,
that husky, breath-loosened laughter learned in back seats and
grocery aisles, the kind that rounds its own edges because it has
no idea what grief costs yet. The laugh did not arrive in his
ears. It arrived in his chest, quick and whole, and was gone
before it had a chance to grow into anybody's face.

He did not chase it. The flood kept coming.

The mitten brushed his knee. He put his palm to it as one
would to the forehead of a fevered child, and it left him the
phantom pressure of a small throb - panic found, panic soothed
- along with the taste of citrus laid open by a thumbnail, and
the chunk of oranges settling into a bin he could not see. A
name rose and struck the back of his teeth. He did not say it.
The wave moved on.

He stepped forward and his footprints kept their radiance. They
brightened again when the water crossed them, and for a
moment the notion of time seemed like a clumsy tool he was
finally allowed to set down. Here, the past did not recede from
the present; it illuminated it. The ground did not forget his
weight; it rewarded it.

When the key drifted close, he lifted it from the inward current
without entirely lifting it at all. The metal did its small familiar
lie about heat - how brass keeps a body's warmth even after the

body has gone. It was no longer stamped 314. The numbers paled and thinned in his hand until they were only the memory of numbers. He waited for the corridor to bloom - the humming lights and the vinyl floor, the counting - 313 - and the awakening before the next digit - but the wave touched his wrist and carried the key's weight away. In its place: a click, dry and ceremonial, the sound a lock makes when it decides to stop being a question.

The cracked lens skimmed past like a coin with no country stamped on it. He touched its edge and received the clink of glass on linoleum and the soft, embarrassed apology of a woman who already knew she was leaving. That apology had never been spoken in any room he remembered; here the room spoke it for her, then closed its mouth.

He took another step. The water traveled deeper onto the land and did not thin. Far behind him, where the horizon should have been, the blankness continued inventing more shoreline, an inland surf that refused to adopt the ordinary direction of retreat. The world was rolling itself toward him, and in doing so it was revealing the stratum beneath: the sedimentary record of a man's uncarried days.

He knelt.

The ground held him with the patience of a bench worn smooth by bodies that learned too late how to rest. The light pooled around his knees. Another wave arrived, quiet as paper turned in a church. He let it pass, and a small plastic keychain kissed the heel of his palm then disappeared - leaving him the humid, humming aisle of a supermarket, his forearm cold from leaning on a refrigeration case, and a laugh that might have been his wife's, or might have been a cheaper version of joy he had mistaken for her voice. He almost smiled. Then he did not.

The luminous footprints behind him remained. He thought of turning to look for the door, for the rusted frame set into rock and the last honest geometry of the lighthouse dissolving. But that would have made distance again, would have taught the new shore the old trick of forward and back. He had the sense that this place would not punish turning around, only misunderstand it. Better, then, to keep the body sincere: one direction, even if direction had been retired.

Another wave assembled - a band of light filamented with darker threads. Inside it, nearer the surface, a paperclip rolled like a fish hooked on no line. He touched the curve of it and felt a carpet under his knees and the prickle of cheap schoolroom dye through corduroy; a yellow folder on a child's lap; a hum with no tune, only certainty; the question of whether he was someone's father or someone's grandfather or a man stranded between the two; the tilt of his laugh when he chose not to answer. The wave went on. The hum stayed in the air as long as a breath can be held, then faded like chalk dust into sunlight.

He moved with the pull. Not against. Not with. Along. His body learned the mean gait of a man walking beside something that does not believe in sideways. Each time the water reached him, he offered a hand, or the idea of one, and each time a thing disclosed itself briefly, like a face pressed to glass from the other side of a lit room. He did not reach for all of them. Some he let pass because restraint here felt like another kind of ritual, and he had promised himself to keep only the rituals that did not pretend to be doctrine.

A baby's sock feathered the surface and was gone. In its wake: the weightless motion of rocking a car seat with a foot while both hands tried to tie a shoe; the sudden knowledge that you are being watched by someone too small to remember your failure, and so you will not fail; the squeak of a hatchback hinge in weather that wanted to be winter.

A man's leather glove revolved and slipped under. He grazed it and had to sit down again. Shame rose, clean and unornamented, the kind that gets its dignity back by telling the truth so plainly it sounds like weather. He didn't hunt the source. He let the wave carry the shame into the ground where, apparently, the ground stored such things until they turned into silt. He could feel it settling, not resolving. Some things ought not be laundered.

The waves kept writing themselves inland.

He watched how the inward surf altered the land it crossed.
With each pass, the surface learned new contours, as if the
current were remembering the old channels of a riverbed.
Small runnels appeared, then wider, then the implied
parentheses of a stream that had never been allowed to exist. In
those newly wet arcs, more objects shook loose: a torn hymn
page that transmuted before his fingers reached the ragged staff
lines; a pencil sharpener that exhaled a sweetness like sugar left
too long on heat; a doorknob that did not turn but carried the
thin, precise sound of a spoon against glass, trivial and exact,
the kind of sound that foundations are made from without ever
being recognized as such.

He waded until the water felt taller than it was. It never rose
above the knee, but the mind delivered deeper measures. With
that sense came the understanding - simple, almost insulting in
its obviousness - that he was not walking beside an element at
all. He was moving through layers. The sea behaving inland
was only how the place disclosed the fact of stratification;
memory lays itself down in beds: light, heavy, particulate,
whole. He had entered his own cross-section.

He said it aloud, because some realizations prefer to be heard
in a voice even if the voice belongs to the one who needs
convincing.

"I am walking through my mind's sediment."

The far-off response arrived first, as always.
my mind's sediment ... my mind's.
The last shedding the pronoun like an unneeded coat.

A wave with no visible objects crossed his ankles and left him
only the warmth of laundry barely out of its drum, the lawful
static of it, the good weight. He thought of how rarely he had
called anything good while it was happening.

He tried to hurry. The place did not understand that word. His
legs continued with the same measured mercy they had

established on the blank plain before shore. He surrendered to their pace.

In the next inward swell a watch floated, hands stuttering in indecision. He pressed a fingertip to the clouded face and heard time do its small, embarrassed cough - tick - tick - tick - like someone tapping a microphone that cannot quite remember how to convert breath into declaration. The watch went out. The cough stayed.

Beyond him, the shore kept adding itself. The far "inland" brightened. If he looked with a kind of sidewise attention, he could see that what seemed empty was not. There were distances full of movement, but the place refused to set them into foreground or background. Everything belonged to the same plane. It was like reading a page where each line asserted itself as the first.

He realized he had stopped marking the waves. He had stopped measuring their frequency or width, ceased worrying whether they might one day rise past the waist, the chest, the throat. Confidence - not the loud kind, but the inherited sort - had arrived. The body had begun to trust that it could be breathed through.

He thought, not without gentleness: *The Manual never had a section for this.* He could almost feel the book on his worktable - its pages delicately warped from some old damp, its title scrawled without pride - refusing to be held here. The place did not want books. It wanted contact.

Another wave showed him a cassette recorder - and then, before he could touch it, pulled the machine back into whatever pocket in the sediment remembered giving permission. He waited in case the voice would come anyway. It did. Or perhaps the place offered him the memory of it because he had proven himself a careful listener.

You can stop now. It's okay to forget some things.

He stood longer than the sentence required. The water crossed and crossed. He did not play it again. He trusted that here, mercy did not evaporate with repetition.

A bright thread wound through the next swell. He reached calmly and found the red shoelace. When he lifted it, the knot resisted, then reconfigured itself without coming loose. The lace departed. In his palm remained the small heat of a child's foot stamping to prove a shoe was on, and the discipline of a double knot, and the knowledge that wildness needs certain harnesses if it is to keep its wildness. Then even that knowledge thinned, kindly.

He wanted to ask the water questions. Where does it begin? Why this order? Who arranged the drawers? But he kept his mouth shut.

A swell line of marbles appeared - a procession of clear glass globes each with a different breath of color trapped at center. They rolled forward together as if strung. He touched only one. Green threaded through it, the exact shade of a windowpane when light remembers to pass through rather than bounce away. He brought it to his eye out of old habit. The world bent, righted itself, and the marble was gone. His pocket felt briefly heavier, then ordinary again.

He looked behind him at last.

The luminous footprints did not form a line. They had learned some other logic. Where he had paused, they widened and brightened, small ponds of witness. Where he had moved steadily, they thinned. The very first seemed to have gone. He knelt to touch the nearest and the light rose into his fingers like water consenting to be held. He felt a wish - not to go back, but to bless where he had been. He pressed his palm to the surface, and the glow accepted the print, then smoothed itself, unimpressed by the sentiment but not offended either.

Reverence here could be local and still be enough.

He stood. The ground learned his weight again and loved it.

The next surge carried no objects he knew but left him a single word spoken underwater. It was a word he must have used hundreds of times without noticing the way it widens the mouth and makes the tongue feel like a small oar rowing toward someone: stay. The word sounded as all underwater words do - like a vow the river is willing to keep on your behalf even if you can't. He nearly said it back. He saved it instead, not as a rule but as a seasoning.

He studied the shore's invention of itself. What had been flat began to dress in the soft topography of a remembered beach: the suggestion of dunes, the drag of tidegrass against an ankle, the darker ribbon where the water always chooses to set its edge. He understood that none of this was the world pretending at geography to put him at ease. It was the mind demonstrating how it makes room for itself when given permission. Grief had always wanted a beach. The archive had wanted weather.

The inward waves slowed. Or he noticed their slowness more accurately. Between them, the air developed a mild shimmer, and objects began to drift there too, no longer needing water to be carried. A pen turned in nothing, leaving the smell of lavender soap and checks written for amounts the body remembers better than the brain: enough. A plastic key fob tumbled and left the idea of a roadside, the sound of gravel spoken under a tire. The oven's old timer ticked once, inaugurally, and decided not to do its job today.

He walked until the horizon changed its mind about being unreachable. It came to meet him the way a thought comes when finally allowed to arrive.

He stopped.

Not to rest. To recognize.

He was not collecting arrivals. He was walking through layers of what he had entrusted to forgetting. The water's reversed motion was only the visible courtesy that allowed him to notice the deeper work: buried things rising through him with the patience of groundwater.

He lowered his hands. Let them hang. Let the waves reach them on their own terms.

They did.

And this time, when the water passed, it left nothing particular - no laugh, no clink, no sentence. It left only the weight of being a body in a place that had decided to keep him.

He took a step.

The print brightened.

He took another.

The sea answered by rolling farther inland, as if making room - not for his progress, which this world had retired - but for his willingness to remain.

He kept walking, and the shore went on inventing itself beneath him, and the sea - obedient to some older law that the living never quite remember - continued to return home.

The mist thickened until the air had seams. It gathered with purpose, collapsing its formlessness into edges, outlines, the faint geometry of a hallway being born. At first it was only suggestion - the way dawn builds itself out of hesitation - but then the suggestion hardened, and light began to take shape inside the fog.

A corridor unspooled ahead of him, narrow, descending narrowly, and lined on both sides with hanging lanterns. Hundreds of them. Perhaps thousands. They hung in even rows, suspended by no visible chain or hook, each one swaying with the slow rhythm of breath. The air around them smelled faintly of tidewater and extinguished wicks, like the remnants of candles that had once promised guidance but had outlived their religion.

The lanterns held what might have been - paths he had almost taken but abandoned at the threshold of choice.

Each lantern contained water. Not still water - living water, seawater that carried the faint movement of a current despite its enclosure. Tiny eddies spun lazily inside the glass chambers, chasing invisible gravity. The light came not from flame but from the water itself, from the luminescent memory of plankton and moonlight folded together.

When Emory stepped closer, the water inside one lantern clarified. Beneath the shifting light, something floated. Not an object - no, a moment. The sight made him forget to take in air.

He saw a kitchen - his, or near enough to fool tenderness. His wife stood at the counter, hair tied back, sleeves rolled to the elbow, humming a song that did not exist. Not a song he could name, but one he instantly knew had been meant for him, written by some gentle, impossible future. The hum was low, private, the kind made when no one is listening, the kind that carries love without agenda.

He took a step nearer, and the hum grew louder, threading itself around the pitch of the corridor's silence. He reached out, and the lantern flickered. The song fractured, breaking into static, and the image dimmed until his reflection replaced hers.

His face stared back at him, older than he remembered, waterlogged by grief. The flicker steadied when he withdrew his hand. The hum resumed, soft but unfinished. He understood then: the lanterns responded to his attention. They fed on it.

He walked deeper into the corridor.

With each step, the light from the lanterns changed hue - blue, then green, then a dim rose that reminded him of late sun filtered through the lighthouse's stained glass. The descent was slow, the air thickening until breathing felt ceremonial. The walls - if they could be called that - were made of the same substance as the mist, neither solid nor yielding, reflecting just enough of his movement to make him wonder whether he was truly walking forward or only deeper into himself.

He stopped before another lantern. Inside this one, the water spun faster, the current forming spirals that resolved into shapes: a child at the edge of a playground, a small figure turning toward him.

It was Etta - but older, impossibly older. The face of a woman he had never met, composed from possibilities he had never allowed himself to imagine. She was sitting cross-legged on a patch of grass; sunlight bent across her cheek. She looked up at someone outside the frame and laughed. Her laugh was the same as when she was eight yet colored by years she had not lived in his world.

Etta wore whatever age the moment required.

He reached toward the glass, desperate to hold the sound, but as his fingertips neared it, the water darkened. The current froze. Her image blurred, then receded like a rush losing interest.

The lantern dimmed, and a low warmth spread through his chest - melancholy first, then something simpler. Peace. Letting it fade, he realized, was like loosening a rope that had been cutting circulation for decades. The air around him softened.

The next lantern he approached burned brighter. He peered in and found a version of himself seated at the lighthouse desk, younger by years, his hair still salted with more light than gray. He was writing in the Manual, head bowed, lips moving faintly as though reciting instructions aloud.

But there was something wrong with the scene. The room in the lantern was inverted - the window on the wrong wall, the desk facing east instead of west. His younger self looked up suddenly, as though sensing he was being watched, and their eyes met through the shifting veil of water.

For an instant, Emory felt a jolt of vertigo. It wasn't recognition that unnerved him, but the difference in expression.

The man in the lantern didn't look haunted. He looked content. As if the ritual had never become a cage.

He wanted to step closer, to ask the image what secret it knew that he had forgotten, but his movement made the lantern's glow falter. The light dimmed to a thin blue thread, and his reflection overlaid the other man's face. Both images wavered - two versions of himself, unable to occupy the same memory.

He pulled back. The lantern steadied. His tempo did not.

He understood, dimly, that this corridor was not an archive of events but of possibilities. Each suspended scene was a life that might have happened, a variation preserved by the oceanic logic of memory. The sea never erases anything; it only redistributes.

He continued forward. The corridor sloped downward, narrowing as he went. The light deepened in tone - lanterns pulsing like a slowed heartbeat.

Some of the images inside were comforting: his daughter learning to ride a bike in a street that no longer existed; his wife asleep on the couch, the television casting stripes of color over her face; his own hands steady as they fixed a toy wheel.

Others turned uncanny. A dining table set for two but neither plate disturbed; his own body standing motionless in the rain, waiting for someone who never arrived; Etta again, but this time as a silhouette walking away from the lighthouse, her form fading before it reached the cliff's bend.

He felt the instinct to catalogue - to impose order, label, preserve. But the Manual was gone, and the act of naming felt suddenly profane. Here, words would only fossilize what needed to flow.

He paused beside a lantern that shone brighter than the rest. Inside, the water was perfectly still. He leaned closer and saw himself reflected not as he was but as something transparent, hollowed by light. His own face watched him from within the lantern, and though the mouth moved, the sound came not from the water but from the air around him: a low whisper shaped like his own voice.

"You kept everything, even the things that begged to be lost."

He closed his eyes. The whisper fell apart, and when he looked again, the lantern was dark.

He let it remain so.

The corridor responded to his surrender. The darkness of that single lantern warmed him, a heat spreading outward through the chill air. The mist stirred, as though approving.

He tested the pattern: approaching one lantern and breathing until it dimmed, then passing to the next. Some went out easily, their images dissolving into gray silt. Others resisted. When he tried to extinguish the one holding his wife's vanished face, pain bloomed - a physical ache radiating from his palms. The air seemed to tighten around his ribs, the corridor drawing in breath it refused to release.

He staggered back, gasping, and the lantern flared bright again. The pain vanished instantly, replaced by cold clarity, a single thought suspended in it like plankton under glass: some lights must be left to burn themselves out.

So he walked on, choosing deliberately. Some memories he let fade, feeling their warmth settle into him like small suns. Others he left untouched, their brightness unspent, knowing that pain has its own stewardship.

He descended further.

The lanterns began to sway more heavily, as if disturbed by unseen movement. Their light rippled across the misted walls, and the corridor took on the appearance of being underwater itself - each step deeper a dive, each breath a negotiation.

He lost sense of how long he had been moving. Time here was less a measurement than an agreement. The air thickened, pressing gently against his ears. The faint hum he had heard when first entering the threshold returned, but now it carried melody - a memory of the song his wife had hummed in that first lantern, looping back upon itself.

He followed the sound until the corridor narrowed to a single line of lanterns descending into darkness. He moved among them slowly, passing faces and gestures that blurred into abstraction, the residue of decades too thin to keep their form.

Finally, he reached the end.

The last lantern hung lower than the rest, barely above the ground, its glass clouded by the residue of salt and time. The water inside glowed faintly, the color of morning light filtered through fog. He knelt.

There he was again - himself at the lighthouse desk, older this time, more familiar. His hand moved across the open Manual, the page lit by a beam that seemed to come from nowhere. He was writing, but no ink appeared. The pen's motion left light instead of words, tracing lines that vanished as quickly as they were made.

Emory watched his double write and erase, write and erase, the ritual looped into futility. For a moment, he felt pity - not for the image, but for the version of himself who still believed record-keeping could postpone loss.

He reached out. His hand touched the glass.

The lantern trembled. The ink on the page inside began to appear - not black, but pale gold - letters forming a sentence he had never written yet somehow recognized:

"The act of keeping is how we forget gently."

The words shone once, then unraveled. The lantern's glow faltered, then steadied.

He could extinguish it, he realized. One exhale, one decision, and this would join the others in merciful darkness. But something in him resisted. There was no pain in this one, only the clean ache of recognition.

He left it burning.

When he stood and took a step beyond, the corridor shivered. The line of lanterns trembled in unison, their waters vibrating as though struck by a single low note. The light flickered from one end to the other like a breath moving through a wind chime.

Then, quietly, the lanterns began to go out ... those that remained lit.

Not by his choice, but by their own.
The extinguishing rolled down the corridor like a slow eclipse, each lantern dimming after the other until the space filled with the deep, soft dark of the ocean floor.

He looked back once. The last light to fade was the one that held him writing. It flickered, folded inward, and was gone.

In the silence that followed, he felt no fear. The absence of light did not mean loss; it meant completion. The corridor had done what it was built for - it had taught him the ethics of release.

The mist loosened its hold, and the walls began to bleed outward, their form collapsing into air. The lanterns melted into glimmers, the last bubbles of a breath finally exhaled.

Emory stepped forward into the dissolving space.

The ground beneath him softened, becoming again the suggestion of surface. The air smelled faintly yesterday's weather.

He did not look back.

Where the corridor had been, there was now only distance, lit by nothing, heavy with mercy.

And somewhere ahead - quiet, patient, beckoning - the sea resumed its slow inward roll.

The corridor had ended without ending.
The last of the lantern light had folded into itself like paper accepting a crease, and the mist had closed behind him, erasing both passage and purpose. The air ahead was dense again, neither black nor luminous - an equilibrium of near-light, as though the world had forgotten how to decide between being visible and being known.

Emory walked until the act of walking no longer changed anything. The ground did not resist or respond; it merely allowed. He felt the texture of his own breath in the air - quiet evidence that he had not entirely unspooled.

Then something shifted.

At first he thought it was his reflection returning - some fragment of the lantern corridor reasserting itself - but the movement held its own gravity. The mist thickened, drew inward, and shaped a silhouette in front of him. The outline sharpened, resolving into a man.

The man was translucent, as if his body had been made from the residue of light left behind when glass forgets what it once held. But the face -
The face was his own.

Younger. Sharper-eyed. The kind of face that still expected the world to answer its questions.

The figure stood a few paces away, hands clasped behind its back, studying him with the calm precision of a scholar examining a specimen that has outlived its classification.

When it spoke, the voice sounded not in the air but within him - an internal resonance, equal parts remembered and unfamiliar.

"You came farther than I expected."

Emory swallowed, the taste of sea still faint on his tongue. "I kept walking."

The figure tilted its head. "That was never the instruction."

"I wasn't given any."

A soft smile flickered across the translucent face. "You were. You simply mistook them for choices."

The silence that followed was not empty; it was crowded with reverberations of their shared timbre, phrases overlapping faintly, as though every word produced its own commentary from the other side of hearing.

Finally, Emory said, "Who are you?"

The figure's smile thinned, becoming something like pity. "I am what remained when you started keeping."

"I don't understand."

"I am the Archivist," the figure said. "The first one. Or perhaps the only one. It hardly matters. I tended this place long before you arrived. I built its drawers. I numbered its absences. I kept the silence alphabetized."

Emory felt a tremor in the air, a small ticking beneath his ribs that could have been recognition or dread. "Then why am I here?"

The Archivist's eyes brightened - no pupils, only rings of pale light turning inward. "Because you mistook the invitation. You were never meant to cross and remain."

The words struck him like cold air through open windows. "The Manual said ..."

"The Manual speaks in possibilities, not permissions," the Archivist interrupted gently. "You were to tend the boundary, not test it. Caretakers preserve what others forget. They do not trespass into the forgetting itself."

Emory felt the quiet sting of reprimand, but beneath it a strange calm. "Then what happens now?"

"That depends on what you seek."

He looked around them, if "around" had any meaning here. The space was infinite and close all at once, walls suggested only by the faint reverberation of their voices. "I want to understand what this is."

"This," the Archivist declared, gesturing to the air, "is what remains when memory runs out of places to live. You have turned forgetting into architecture."

He stepped closer, and their outlines blurred where they overlapped, one form inside the other, like ripples colliding in still water. "You called yourself the first Archivist. What does that make me?"

The figure's tone softened. "You were the caretaker."

"And you?"

"I was the kept."

The remnant of the moment hung there, vibrating gently between them.

"You kept yourself," Emory said, realizing the symmetry as he spoke.

The Archivist smiled faintly. "I forgot myself."

Something in that admission - the ease of it, the unburdened surrender - filled Emory with both envy and recognition.

He studied the younger version's face, the unlined certainty in it, the way it seemed almost translucent with conviction. "Were you me once?"

"Names are clumsy here," the Archivist said. "If you need that to be true, let it be. But remember - truth is only what memory refuses to abandon."

They stood in a silence that stretched without time. The mist moved around them in slow, deliberate currents, responding to breath rather than wind.

After a while, Emory asked, "Why do you look younger?"

"Because you remember yourself most clearly in the years before you learned to doubt what remembering costs."

The response landed somewhere beneath logic, true not because it made sense, but because it felt inevitable.

The Archivist stepped past him, pacing with the same unhurried rhythm Emory had once used to circle the Archive Room. "You think this is discovery. It is repetition. Every keeper eventually follows his own trail inward until he mistakes it for a road. You reached the point where memory turned inward, and you called it a door. It was not. It was a mirror."

Emory turned. "Then what is beyond the mirror?"

"Nothing you can own."

The figure stopped walking and faced him again. "Tell me ... what do you intend to find beyond this place?"

Emory hesitated. He thought of the lanterns, the inverted sea, the objects that had lost contour beneath his touch. Each revelation had peeled something from him, each release both mercy and diminishment. He felt hollowed but not empty - a vessel newly aware of its shape.

He met the Archivist's gaze and said, quietly, "Whatever remains after names."

The figure's expression changed, first to surprise, then to something closer to tenderness. "Ah," it said, almost to itself. "Then you've begun to understand."

The mist around them shifted. It wasn't wind - it was breath, slow and deliberate. The space inhaled.

The Archivist stepped closer, and as he did, the edges of his form began to fray, threads of light unraveling from his arms, his hair, the outline of his jaw. The translucence deepened until Emory could see through him entirely - past him, into the slow thread of the horizon that had no source.

"You cannot stay here," the Archivist said. "You are written into this place now, line by line, object by object. If you remain, you will solidify. You will become another drawer in the Archive."

"What must I do?"

The smile returned, faint as a reflection on still water. "To proceed, you must unwrite."

"I must lessen so you may rise."

Those phrases drifted between them, not as instruction, but as invitation. The Archivist raised a hand and something small appeared in his palm - a page, yellowed, edges trembling as though resisting disappearance.

Emory stepped forward to take it, but the Archivist's fingers opened and the page floated upward, turning over itself as it rose. On its surface, faint lines of text appeared, written backward - mirror-script, shimmering in reverse.

The air hummed around them. The letters shifted until they caught the light just right, and for an instant, Emory could read them:

To proceed, unwrite.

He looked up, but the Archivist was already unraveling, his outline blurring into the mist.

"Wait," Emory said. "If I unwrite myself - what remains?"

The voice that answered him came from everywhere and nowhere, woven through the air like a living thing.

"What remains," it said, "is what never needed writing."

And then he was gone.

He faded not in defeat but in completion - the first keeper released by the next.

The space he left behind did not close. It simply forgot to contain itself, expanding until even absence felt crowded. The page drifted downward, slow as ash in still air.

Emory reached for it. The paper was warm - not with heat, but with the movement of recognition. The mirrored script shimmered against his skin, and as he traced the backward letters with his thumb, they began to dissolve, each one sinking into his skin like ink returning to the hand that had spilled it.

He closed his fist around the vanishing page. When he opened it again, nothing remained.

Only the faint impression of words pressed into his palm - indentations without ink.

He looked around. The mist had thinned. Through it, he could see faint outlines - layers of the world superimposed, half-formed and trembling. The waves rolling inward, the shore still glowing with his footprints, the faint afterimage of the lantern corridor behind him, all coexisting in impossible simultaneity.

And beneath it all, he sensed writing. Not on surfaces, but within them - threads of script woven through the fabric of the air, the ground, his own skin. Every object, every moment, every loss had been transcribed into the world like a sentence.

His life was the ink. This place was the paper.

He stood in the silence that followed, understanding dawning slowly and without mercy. If he wanted to move forward - if there was even such a direction here - he would have to erase the record that kept him tethered.

He looked at his hands. They trembled, faintly luminous, already becoming translucent at the edges. The process had begun.

He whispered to the empty air, "To proceed, unwrite."

The mist stirred in answer.

And as he took his first step into the thinning horizon, the undertone of the Archivist's final smile lingered -
a warmth without face,
a forgiveness without form.

Somewhere, behind and within him, the sound of the sea exhaled.

It sounded almost like a page turning.

Part Three – The Sea

The air grew heavier before the ground began to slope. The horizon folded in on itself, the light flattening until everything shimmered like the surface of still water under a clouded sky. When Emory took another step, the terrain became indistinct beneath him, and he was descending. Not falling - lowering, as though the world were gently pouring him into its next chamber.

The smell of the brine arrived first - thick, ancient, immediate. It was not the sharp tang of open ocean but the deeper scent of something mined: grief compacted until it crystallized. The mist thinned and the new space took shape, vast and subterranean, illuminated by its own quiet luminescence.

He stood in a hall made entirely of salt.

The walls glowed faintly, granular veins catching the dim blue of unseen light. Salt ridged the floor like cooled lava, brittle and uneven, crackling faintly beneath his steps. The air felt charged, as though it remembered storms. And lining the hall, stretching into vanishing perspective, were shelves - endless, regimented, perfect.

Each shelf was carved directly from the salt.
Each held jars.

The jars were different. These were not possibilities. These were the years he had actually carried.

Thousands of them, maybe millions - glass jars sealed with wax, their bellies full of seawater. The shelves receded into the mist in both directions like the ribs of a sleeping leviathan, disappearing where the light ran out. Every jar had a small, uneven label pressed into the salt above it. The handwriting was his own.

He stepped closer. The first label read: 1969.
The next: 1972.
After that, 1985, 1986, 1990, and then a gap where the years should have continued. A foggy span of shelving where no labels could be read, as if memory had grown embarrassed of chronology.

He touched one of the jars. Its glass was cool, sweating faintly as though it held a temperature different from the world around it. The water inside shimmered faintly, rippling with unseen movement. He leaned closer and saw -
Not reflection. Not distortion.
A scene.

Within the jar, impossibly small, a day unfolded.

A boy - himself at ten - sat on the cracked wooden dock behind his childhood home, legs dangling over the water, a book open on his knees. The light was early morning, patient and gold. Somewhere behind him, a woman's voice called his name. His mother's, but younger. The boy turned but did not answer. He was tracing his finger along a line of text in the book, mouthing words with an intensity that had nothing to do with understanding.

Emory reached forward, mesmerized. The scene moved as he moved, the water bending light around memory. He unscrewed the wax-sealed lid, just by a hair's width.

The sound arrived all at once.

The rustle of wind through reeds. The creak of the dock's timbers. A woman calling again - closer this time, more insistent. The smell of river mud, of sun-warmed wood. And the taste of orange peel, bitter and sweet, lingering on a child's tongue.

The air around him swelled, full of living sound, until the pressure forced him back. Then the jar shuddered in his hand. The water within it darkened, cloudy as grief. The voices thinned into static, then silence. He tried to replace the lid, but the seal had dissolved. The jar emptied itself, a thin stream of sea-marrow running over his fingers and onto the salt floor.

Where it touched, the salt hissed softly, like something waking.

When he set the jar down again, its label had faded to blank.

He stared at it for a long time, feeling the residual warmth on his hand. The grief wasn't sharp. It was fine-grained, like powder, settling into every fold of him.

He continued walking.

The years leapt and stuttered. 1974. 1978. 1982.
Some sections of shelving were full; others were gaps, the shelves bare, their surfaces fogged as though something invisible had been taken.

When he brushed the empty spaces, his fingertips came away wet.

He reached 1985 and stopped. That label alone seemed to glow faintly, as if underlined by memory itself. The jar there was larger, the glass thicker, the water restless.

He lifted it down with both hands, careful but unafraid. The label wavered beneath his thumb: *August 1985 - the day of the storm.*

The water inside wasn't clear. It spun with suspended silt, flashes of lightning woven into the bitter water. He unscrewed the lid.

Rain hit instantly - impossible rain, heavy and warm, falling inside his lungs instead of on his skin. He was back on the beach, holding his daughter's hand, her small body shaking with the thrill of thunder. The storm was coming in too fast. His wife was shouting something from the car. He could taste ocean spray and fear at once. And then the moment inverted: the child was gone, the shoreline empty, his own voice calling her name against the wind.

The sound built until it nearly broke him. He clamped the lid shut. The rain stopped.

Inside the jar, the storm calmed, clouds settling into amber haze. The water cleared until nothing was visible but faint motion at its core, the heartbeat of a wave that refused to die.

He returned it to the shelf, hand shaking. The label now read only: *Etta.*

He backed away, breathing shallow. The air was thicker now, humid with drift. His mouth tasted of iron and sorrow.

He walked on. The labels jumped forward - 1992. 1998. 2003. 2008. 2010.

The missing years were numerous, their absence louder than any presence. It struck him that these gaps might not represent forgotten times, but the ones he had chosen not to revisit.

He ran his hand along the jars as he passed. Some hummed faintly under his touch. Others recoiled, their water stilling like held breath.

He stopped at 2010. The jar there was smaller, its glass faintly cracked. The water inside was almost still, only a single swirl of light moving within it, slow as smoke.

He didn't remember 2010. Not specifically. The year felt like a
closed room. He uncapped it anyway.

The air filled with the smell of antiseptic, followed by a sharp
beep. Hospital light. Vinyl flooring. His mother's face, worn
but lucid, eyes bright with recognition and disappointment.
She was saying his name.
Then another sound - a door opening somewhere he couldn't
see. Nurses moving quickly.
A voice, younger and male, his own, saying, *Tell her I'll come
tomorrow.*

The sound fractured.
Her breathing hitched once, twice - then the jar cracked in his
hands.

He sealed it, but it was too late. The memory drained, and he
felt its loss physically - a pressure behind the sternum, as
though the air had been drawn out of him. The crack in the jar
ran all the way down, the seam of a wound refusing to close.

He set it back on the shelf. The label bled its ink until it read
nothing at all.

He pressed his forehead against the cool wall of salt.
"I didn't mean to forget," he whispered.
The hall did not answer.
But the salt beneath his breath glittered faintly, and a thin,
crystalline tear slid down the wall, freezing halfway through its
fall.

The wall learned handwriting.

Salt lifted itself into script directly above the shelf where he'd
set the broken year. Letters brightened, then held, as if they had
been waiting under the surface for breath.

Open three, it said.

Another line formed beneath it, thinner, almost embarrassed to
be read: and three will unname you.

He did not move.

Around him, the long aisles kept their patient glow, but one section of racking leaned - barely, like a tired shoulder - and seven jars answered the tilt by brightening from within. No years on their labels. Only nouns pressed into the salt above each: *Child, Husband, Son, Keeper, Penitent, Witness, Friend.*

He wanted to open them all. Not from greed. From the old superstition that enough could be learned if he just lifted one more lid.

Somewhere in the hall a thin, ceremonial beep repeated - three times, then silence - as if the world were counting to a small rule.

He reached toward *Keeper* and, as his hand moved, something else appeared - five chalk-white letters raised out of the salt like dry bones: E   M   O   R   Y. The name wasn't carved in one place; it had distributed itself along the shelf-edge labels, a letter here, a letter there, the way weather distributes a thought across a cliff.

He lifted *Keeper*.

The glass stayed cool. The water within it turned once, like a thought deciding, and a draft moved through the hall with the sound of paper unlearning ink. When the moment released him, the E on the shelf faded, smudged by no hand - only light.

He set the jar back. His upper body answered with that small pressure that arrives when a room tells a story without raising its voice.

Open three, the salt repeated, the line brighter now, and the ceiling gave a slow, crystalline sigh - loosening its grip in a fine powder he could taste.

He took *Witness* next.

It smelled of rain on unpainted wood and a throat clearing in the dark before a sentence that never quite begins. He saw himself at a distance, doing nothing wrong and nothing brave, and the room forgave him for both. When the jar's sound thinned, the M on the labels dulled to the color of breath on glass.

Two letters left themselves bright.

He understood, without needing it explained, that the letters of his name were not decoration but tether. If they disappeared, so would his claim to the world waiting ahead. Whatever door the number was meant to open would forget to open for him.

A corridor would remain a corridor. A door would remember only how to be a wall.

He steadied himself and looked again at the glowing, untouched five - each jar alive with its own small persuasion.

Child, bright as a supernova.
Husband, giving off a low, domestic warmth.
Penitent, its lid warped by long patience.
Friend, humming faintly, the sound a room makes when it approves of your arrival.
Son, quiet as a kept photograph, the kind you never frame because you already know it by heart.

He took *Penitent*.

The seal lifted with a soft refusal, then yielded. Warmth crossed his face as if a hand had been raised there once and did not fall. A sentence rose and did not finish; that was enough. When he set the jar down, the O on the labels thinned to a mere habit of a circle.

Above him, a few grains let go from the ceiling - slow snow, nothing more - but he could feel the hall's geometry beginning to keep time.

"Not all," he said to the room, not bargaining, only confessing his arithmetic.

At that, the script wavered. The first line - *open three* - dimmed to a kind of permission, and the second - and three will unname you - softened until the letters became texture and then salt again.

The seven jars eased back into the common light, their glow ordinary as other years. On the shelf-faces, his name resumed itself faintly - not fully restored, not lost - like tide marks that prefer to be read by touch.

He stood very still and let the room finish deciding. No more beeps. Only the low hush of this place doing its work.

When he turned from that leaning section, his body had learned a small caution that did not feel like fear. To open is to pay. To pay is to proceed.

He kept moving.

As he went, he began opening jars deliberately.
One by one.
He stopped reading labels.

Each one contained a day - a breakfast, an argument, a letter, a silence.

Each release filled the room with a brief, overwhelming reality: the smell of coffee that morning his wife had finally smiled again; the sound of a radio half-tuned to static; the taste of soap from washing Etta's mouth when she'd cursed for the first time; the laughter that had followed anyway.

And each time, when the scene collapsed, his body flickered, faintly luminous. His hands blurred at the edges. He was unwriting himself in small increments, trading flesh for memory.

The jars responded in kind. The more he opened, the louder the hall became - a cacophony of voices, overlapping and contradicting, all his own but fractured across decades.

Some spoke in tones of apology. Others in laughter. Some only breathed.

He walked through the growing noise like a man crossing the surf, buffeted but steady. The air itself grew liquid.

He opened one labeled 1972.
The scent of chalk dust and pencil shavings rose around him. A classroom. The hum of a fluorescent light.
He was twelve, sitting by a window, carving his initials into the wooden desk. Outside, rain. Inside, the ache of being unseen.
He opened another - 1998.
He was at a grocery store, arguing with his wife about something unimportant. The cashier watching, pretending not to. The moment afterward, in the car, the apology neither of them said.

He opened 1978. The day of his father's funeral. The silence after the sermon, when everyone had left.
He opened 2003. The first Christmas after the separation. The same meal, cooked for one.

He stopped counting the years. The chronology collapsed. Time became an ocean made of rooms.

The jars emptied themselves, their brine soaking into the salt floor. The ground hissed and glittered with each release, the way fire sometimes whispers before smoke claims the rest.

He was dissolving. He knew it.

Every time a jar's lid left his hand, his fingers lost a little of their certainty, turning translucent like glass in fog. His reflection on the salt walls flickered - solid, then spectral, then gone.

Still, he kept opening.

There was a strange peace in the unmaking. Each unraveled moment felt less like loss and more like translation, as though he was being rewritten in a language with no words.

When at last he reached the far end of the hall, the shelves began to slope upward again. The air grew colder, cleaner. Only a few jars remained. The labels had lost sequence entirely: Unknown. Unfiled. Untitled.

He took one down. The jar was small, the wax seal uneven, as though applied in haste. Inside, the water was perfectly still. He hesitated, then removed the lid.

Nothing happened. No sound, no scent, no image.
Only the feeling of standing inside the moment after something has ended but before anyone knows it has.

Then he understood: this jar was tomorrow. The day that hadn't yet written itself.

He replaced the lid gently, and as he did, he caught sight of his own reflection in the water - pale, fragmented, half-absent. Light passed through him like sunlight through shallow surf.

He was almost gone.

All around him, the shelves had begun to lose form, their minerals running in rivulets down the walls. The jars melted into themselves, their glass merging with the mire. The air filled with the scent of ocean and endings - the dense perfume of grief when it finally exhales.

He turned once, taking in the vastness of the Library as it collapsed. Each dissolving jar whispered as it went, a sibilant chorus:
Remember... remember...
But the word no longer meant what it once had.

He realized, suddenly, that memory was not the act of keeping, but the act of *releasing carefully enough that it leaves a shape behind.*

He stepped forward. The floor cracked beneath him, the sound bright as ice breaking on a river.

His hand glowed faintly as he lifted it to his chest. The beat there was slow, tidal. Each sequence carried salt through him, the body learning at last to become what it had always resisted - part sea, part silence.

He reached the ascending ramp and paused. Behind him, the Library had become a vast, shimmering pool, all shelves and jars blurred into liquid light.

For a moment, it looked as though the entire room were breathing.

He whispered to it, his voice nearly transparent. "Thank you."

The surface rippled, once. Then stilled.

When he turned to climb, his footprints left behind no glow this time. Only wetness. And as he moved upward into the waiting mist, his reflection did not follow.

It stayed in the salt, dissolving last, the final remnant of a man who had opened himself until nothing remained but light suspended.

And far above, beyond the weight of the earth, the sea inhaled, drawing back the scent of itself - salt and paper and everything he had once been.

The sound reached him before the light returned.
A low, tuneless hum, almost shy in its persistence - the kind of sound a child makes when the world feels too quiet and she decides to fill it.

It came from somewhere inside the collapse.

Emory turned toward it. The Library of Salt continued its unmaking of itself, the shelves melting into luminous runoff that trickled across the ground in rivulets. The air was thick

with the mineral scent of dissolution, like rain on old bones.
Yet through the hiss and murmur of dissolving salt, the
humming stayed steady, stubborn, perfectly pitched against the
decay.

He followed the sound, stepping carefully through the shallow
sea-slurry pooling around his ankles. His reflection fragmented
in the liquid - flashes of a man only intermittently solid, the
rest a trembling mirage.

The humming grew clearer as he descended through what
remained of the hall. The light had shifted to that pale, dusty
gold that doesn't belong to any hour. The walls flickered
between stone and air, between now and memory.

And then he saw her.

She sat at a small wooden desk in the middle of what had once
been the central aisle of the Library - a child, maybe eight
years old, bent over a piece of paper. The desk itself was a
strange construction, assembled from driftwood, smooth and
salt-bleached, held together by copper nails greened with
corrosion. The child's feet did not reach the floor. Her legs
swung idly in rhythm with the hum.

Etta.

Not the ghost of her, not a vision softened by distance.
Simply her. The girl as she had been - hair parted degrees off-
center, a smudge of blue crayon on her left hand, the same
defiant tilt of chin that always seemed halfway between
curiosity and accusation.

On the desk before her lay a page torn from some long-
vanished workbook. She was coloring a picture of a lighthouse,
though the colors defied reason: the tower's walls a bright
green, the sea below it a calm shade of rust.

He stood a few paces away, afraid that moving closer might
disrupt the fragile geometry of her existence.

"Etta," he said softly.

She didn't look up. Her crayon scraped across the page, filling the outline of a wave with slow, deliberate strokes. "You were late again."

The words landed gently, but they hollowed him all the same.

He tried to speak, but the apology came out as breath instead of sound. The air between them absorbed it, indifferent.

She kept coloring. "You said you'd come to the play. You promised."

Emory swallowed. The memory surfaced unbidden - an auditorium half-full of folding chairs, his wife in the second row, their daughter onstage in cardboard wings. He had been at work then, too tired to remember, too proud to call. The guilt had faded over the years until it felt like a smudge rubbed almost clean. But hearing it again in her voice - small, matter-of-fact - reopened the wound with surgical precision.

"I'm sorry," he said, his voice finally catching.

"That's what you said last time," she replied, still not looking up. "But sorry is just a kind of story, isn't it? You tell it so you don't have to remember."

"You are someone's dad."

He took a hesitant step closer. The ocean's lace rippled around his feet. "You're real," he whispered.

"Of course I am." She switched crayons, now using yellow to fill the lighthouse beam, though it radiated in impossible directions - downward, sideways, spiraling inward instead of out. "Everything you forgot had to go somewhere. Someone had to keep it."

Her words were calm, but they carried the gravity of an inheritance.

He wanted to touch her, to confirm the warmth of her skin, but when he reached out, his hand passed through her shoulder as though she were made of water. His fingers tingled with the cold residue of contact denied.

She sighed, but it wasn't disappointment - more like patient acknowledgment of a rule she hadn't written. "You don't belong on this side anymore. Not really."

The driftwood creaked softly beneath her as she leaned forward, concentrating on her drawing. "Do you know what I'm doing?"

He shook his head.

"I'm cataloguing you," she said. "The way you used to catalogue everything else."

She pointed to the paper, and only then did he notice that the lighthouse she'd drawn wasn't some imagined tower - it was his. The old lighthouse, the one above the cliff. Every line of its weathered stone was rendered with childish precision. Around it, she had drawn waves that looked more like words, curling script too small to read.

Each wave was a sentence. Each sentence, a day.

She continued, her voice soft but precise. "You kept everything that wasn't meant to be kept - the guilt, the lingerings, the noise. I'm just putting it back where it belongs."

He felt a weight in his torso, the slow tightening of air that accompanies recognition. "You're not supposed to be here," he said.

"Neither are you," she answered. "But you came anyway. You always do."

He knelt beside her, though the floor seemed to shift beneath him, alternately solid and liquid. "Etta, please. Tell me what happens now."

At that, she finally looked up.

Her face flickered - child, adult, stranger - each version overlapping like reflections seen through water. The transitions were seamless yet jarring: her eyes would age while the rest of her stayed young; her hair would gray, then darken again. She looked like the entire arc of her life compressed into a single moment of seeing.

"What happens now," she said, "is what's already happened. You'll keep remembering until you disappear."

He wanted to argue, but there was no room for denial here. The truth had the density of grief; it did not yield to protest.

She smiled faintly, that same uneven smile he remembered from her childhood - half joy, half challenge. "Don't look so worried. I'm not angry anymore."

"I was supposed to protect you," he said. "And instead ..."

"You tried," she interrupted gently. "That's what people forget when they talk about failure. Trying is still a kind of love."

He felt tears rise but couldn't tell if they were made of water or light. "I never stopped loving you."

"I know," she said simply. "Love is the undercurrent that never learned to retreat."

For a long moment, neither spoke. The sound of dissolving salt filled the space like soft applause.

On her desk sat a small glass marble. It was clear with a green thread spiraling through its center - identical to the one he carried. The light from it flared faintly, in rhythm with his own heartbeat.

Etta picked it up and rolled it between her palms, studying it. "You left this behind once," she said. "It rolled under the couch, and you never looked for it. I found it years later, but by then you'd forgotten it existed."

She placed it on the desk and nudged it toward him. It rolled slowly across the wood, humming faintly, until it reached the edge and stopped, balanced perfectly before falling.

He hesitated, then reached out. When his fingers brushed it, something inside his chest shifted - a small, clean realignment, like the click of a key finding its lock. The marble sank through his skin and vanished into him. His body glowed faintly for an instant, then steadied.

Etta smiled again, satisfied. "Now you're whole enough to keep walking."

He wanted to thank her, but gratitude felt too small a currency. Instead, he asked, "Why me? Why all this?"

"Because you cared too much about what was gone," she said. "You kept the world from moving on. So it sent me to keep you."

She looked down at her drawing again, her crayon moving more slowly now, tracing the outline of the lighthouse beam. "But don't stay too long. The salt eats names here."

She looked past him toward the slow-forming city where the dissolving shelves had begun to arrange themselves into streets.

"Someone's caught," she said.

He followed her gaze.

Near the fountain of turning pages, a small forgetting - child-shaped, bright at the edges - struggled to move. Only one shoe. The other foot was bare, stalled halfway in air, as if the world had forgotten how to finish drawing it.

Etta set down her crayon. "It can't leave like that. You know what to do."

"I don't," he said.

"You do. You've always known how to hold on. Now learn the opposite."

She reached toward his breastbone, not touching, just indicating the center where the word had always lived. "Find one word you still keep. Give it to the fountain. That's the price."

"What word?"

"The one you reach for when you beg the world not to change."

He understood at once. The word had followed him through every silence, every loss. It had lived in his throat even when prayer had gone mute.

Stay.

He looked at the trapped forgetting - its outline flickering like wet paper held to a flame - and felt the old reflex rise: to rescue, to keep, to insist.

The salt air pressed at his skin. The choice tightened like a knot.

He bent, lifted the child's small outline by its hand, and led it toward the fountain. The pages turned slowly, waterless yet moving as though reciting something too old to forget.

Etta watched from the desk, silent.

When they reached the edge, he felt the word land inside his mouth, eager and afraid. He cupped it as if it were water.
The syllable trembled against his palm.

He bent to the fountain. "Stay," he whispered.

The word left him with the lightness of breath and the weight of a vow breaking. The fountain brightened; its pages fluttered once, pleased. A second shoe appeared on the child's foot. The silhouette smiled - or maybe the light smiled through it - and then it was gone, surrender cleanly into air.

He staggered back, throat raw though he'd spoken only once.

Etta's voice reached him, soft as surf. "Now it's gone from you."

He tried to repeat the word, to test it, but nothing came. Only air, shaped but soundless.

He touched his lips, astonished at the emptiness there. "I can't ..."

"You won't need to," she said. "The world remembers it for you."

The fountain's glow dimmed. Somewhere in the city, a thousand quiet footsteps resumed their motion, balanced again.

He frowned. "What does that mean?"

Her voice softened, almost a whisper. "You can love a thing and still need to let it vanish."

The words struck with the gentle finality of an amen.

She turned the page over, revealing a new sheet beneath it - blank, waiting. "You'll need this one later," she said.

He wanted to ask what she meant, but the question broke apart before leaving his mouth. The world around them was shifting again. The Library's remnants were liquefying, turning the floor into a shallow sea. The driftwood desk began to float, rocking faintly as if on a calm stream.

Etta kept drawing. The crayon's movement left no color now, only light. Each stroke etched a faint glow into the air that lingered even after the paper yielded. The glow formed shapes - outlines of doors, of waves, of paths leading upward.

He realized she wasn't drawing anymore. She was writing him out.

"Etta," he said softly, "don't."

She paused, looking up at him again, her face now stable, purely herself - the eight-year-old with the blue crayon stain on her hand. "You've been here long enough," she said. "You don't belong in the remembering anymore."

Her tone was neither cruel nor kind. It was factual, the way truth sometimes is when spoken by those who have outgrown their pain.

He reached for her again, but his hand passed through the air above her shoulder, scattering faint motes of light like disturbed dust. The contact that wasn't left a cold ache in his chest.

"I'll see you again," he said.

She shook her head gently. "Not like this."

She hums an ancient prayer, one that felt older than speech:

"Return him to the turning,
keep him in the sound.
Let the water take his shadow,
but leave the light he found.
What drifts away is gathered,
what breaks will learn to mend.
The sea begins where memory ends."

The desk began to drift backward, the water deepening beneath her. She didn't seem afraid. She kept humming that same familiar tune - the one from the classroom. The sound folded into the dissolving world like fabric into flame.

"Don't stay too long," she repeated, her voice now distant but still clear. "The salt eats names."

Then the light around her flared - a soft, blinding radiance like morning sun breaking through fog. When it faded, the desk was gone. The water was calm. The only thing that remained was the faint outline of a drawing, burned into the surface of the world: a lighthouse drawn by a child, its beam turning inward, endlessly illuminating the place where memory and love had learned, finally, to let each other go.

Emory stood in the stillness, the marble's warmth pulsing faintly inside him. He could feel her humming somewhere beneath the surface of the water, a vibration stitched into the rhythm of his own heartbeat.

He whispered, "I'll remember," though he knew the promise would not last.

Then he turned toward the fading path she had drawn in light and began to walk, each step dissolving a little more of the man he had been - not as punishment, but as passage.

And in the silence that followed, the sea exhaled, tasting his name one final time before beginning to forget it.

The first water did not come from the ground.
It came from the books that did not exist.

Where shelves had stood, where salt had remembered how to hold the weight of glass, the Library's faint after-architecture quivered - as if realizing, too late, that it had been a body all along. The seams of the world opened along their quietest lines: between vein and vein of salt, between a shelf and the idea of a shelf, between a label and the year it had once convinced into staying. From those fine and faultless places, droplets formed.

They beaded without hurry, round and perfectly self-possessed, as if water had always been the library's true script and was merely resuming its sentence.

The first droplet fell.
It struck the dissolving floor with a sound that could have been a word and might have been. Then another. A staccato of beginnings. Emory stood very still and listened.

Each drop whispered something as it let go.

Not through the ear - through the air itself, the way heat announces itself to skin. He felt them more than heard them: half-confessions, old refusals softened by time, the throat-clearing of apologies that never learned their final shape. Between them, fragments of the Manual surfaced and sank, pale as fish in silt.

Dust the objects.
Catalog any new arrivals in the Register of Apparitions.
Never throw anything away.
Never ask who they belonged to.

Then a voice that was not instruction: his mother's - lucid, tired, fond in a way that warmed and reprimanded at once.
You are not late if you arrive at the only hour that will forgive you.

The droplets quickened. A soft rain, inside. The hall took the sound into itself and made a chorus no one had rehearsed. Emory raised his face to it. The water carried no temperature, only weight - the kind of weight that teaches a body to bow without shame.

Out of habit, out of gratitude, he reached for a lantern.

He had not brought one. Yet when he lifted his hand, it was there - unbroken glass and seawater's slow intelligence cradled in his palm. Light leaked from it without brightness, more posture than illumination. It swung in his grip with the patience of a metronome. He understood: the corridor had given it back not as an object, but as permission. A carried horizon.

He started forward.

The library - the memory of it - widened and thinned as if distance had nothing to do with space and everything to do with willingness. Where rows had been, water now threaded itself along capillaries in the salt, waking a riverbed that had never been allowed to declare itself. The shelves loosened into shorelines. The labels, stubborn as old vows, blurred to pale hyphens and slid away.

He waded. The sludge reached his ankles, then his calves, then held there as if negotiating a treaty. Each step forced light into the water. He watched his shins through the flood: a man's legs becoming the idea of legs, then becoming the memory of the idea - refracted, resolved, let go.

From the walls, another sentence fell, spoken in the even tone of a woman accustomed to reading aloud to keep a room calm. *You kept the world. You did not let it keep you.*

His mother again - or the place borrowing her to make its case.

He did not answer. Answers were a way of throwing a rope around a thing that needed wind.

The lantern's glow, such as it was, softened the words until they lost their edges and went to ground. The Manual fragments returned, now less command than response.

Catalog ...

Never throw anything away.

Emory smiled with a fatigue that felt older than bone. "You were wrong about that," he told the air, and the air, relieved, did not disagree.

The water rose a fraction. It did not surge. It reasoned. It set itself against the walls and waited until the stone admitted the argument. Salt gave way in small, resigned sighs, glittering where it yielded, shining in humiliation that was not humiliation at all - only completion.

A droplet struck his shoulder and unraveled into syllables as it fell: *Stay.*

He remembered the word as he had heard it underwater in the reversed surf, the way it widens the mouth and resembles a plea even when it is only a small domestic hope. The lantern trembled in his hand and steadied. The syllable unthreaded as it touched the glass, as if the world had learned at last not to record everything.

He moved deeper. Where the long wall should have turned, it leaned instead, as if braced against a pressure no blueprint could predict. From its porous surface, lines of water webbed outward and downward, and from each thread came a sentence mid-habit:

I'll come tomorrow.
Just a moment, stay close.
Tell her I'll call back.
This time, I will.

Half-honest, half-kind. He loved them for trying.

He held the lantern higher. Its light did not strike the words so much as befriend them. They loosened, the way a clenched hand relinquishes its small, righteous ache. They ran to the floor and joined the accumulating sea. Where they disappeared, the architecture evaporated - a bracket of wall, a quiet corner, an aisle recognized only by how air behaves inside an aisle. Unwritten.

The more the water flooded, the more the library forgot it had ever been a room.

He watched as a section of shelving took on the peaceful tilt of a dune and then relaxed into smoothness. A plank of remembered wood sighed and became the simple logic of tide-flat. Labels unhooked themselves from grammar and returned to salt. The ceiling, which he had not bothered to see, remembered it had been sky once, and then forgot even that, choosing openness over allegory.

Emory's body registered the cost. Each collapse exacted a toll in light. He flickered. Like sunlight tasting the shallow places before it admits its own failure at depth. His forearms thinned first - the edges of him asked to trust that shape is a courtesy rather than a right. The lantern's handle passed through his palm and held anyway, as if the glass preferred the memory of being carried to the fact.

From the wall: a small laugh, unmistakable and from some day with oranges.

It's not the end of the world, a woman said in his direction, the way people say such things when they mean, *please do not make me carry you and the world both.*

The droplet that delivered it swung from stalactites the salt had fashioned in its last vanity. It fell. It made the sentence into rain and the rain into hush.

He waded on. The water was at his knees now, and with it came the softened percussion of footsteps that did not belong to him, not exactly. Not ghosts. Guests. All the versions of himself and his family and their strangers who had learned, under all kinds of weather, to walk in and out of rooms with a decency that nearly redeemed them.

From the left, a seam in the wall unthreaded itself and let go of another voice: the Manual again, exhausted and sincere:
If it pulses, it belongs to you.

"Yes," he said, surprising himself with the gentleness of his agreement. "And if it disappears, I must not chase it."

The lantern answered with a slow brightening that could have been approval. Or memory playing at flame.

He paused. The flood carried small, readable things past his shins: the shape of a ribbon pretending to be a shoelace; a coin that remembered being a lens; a yo-yo that refused to hurry. Each brushed him and melted, leaving sensations that did not obey sequence: a child's breath warming his collarbone from a time she was short enough to live there; the click of a door brought to heel by a key; the delicate clink of a spoon against glass, trivial and exact, the sound that seems to arrive from nowhere and proves a life is happening.

He tipped his head back and let the rain fall into his open mouth. It brought no water - only letters. S, then A, then L, then T. He swallowed them. They tasted like grief learning to be mineral. The word softened into him and named nothing but did not need to.

He understood now: unwriting was literal. The flood was erasure in its kindest form. He had confused keeping with love. The room, in its patience, was teaching him how a storm edits a coastline - without malice, without haste, with a devotion to shapes no map will admit until afterwards.

He walked until the floor ceased to recognize itself as floor. The world beneath his feet became the suggestion of surface again - the same permissive firmness that had received him when he first crossed the threshold. The library's final architecture - arch, aisle, ladder rung, handrail polished by a thousand research afternoons - held a breath as if to defend itself and then exhaled, choosing usefulness over pride. With each exhale, a little more vanishing.

He set the lantern on what had once been a desk. The desk was water now, but water remembers flatness, and the glass bobbed with the decorum of a boat that knows it is in church. He placed his palm beside it and felt the count there, not his heart, but something older in him - what the sea had left behind when it climbed out of its cradle and tried being a man for a while.

He thought he heard, very near, Etta's humming. He did not turn. The humming was the world's way of reminding him the child had done her part. You do not keep a keeper.

From the dissolving wall: his mother again, closer this time, as if leaning in to make sure he received the line clean:
You left things behind so you wouldn't drown.

Then, soft as pity being careful not to condescend:
Now you've learned to breathe under water.

He smiled. The sentence did not lance him as it once would have. It sounded like graduation.

He lifted the lantern and waded toward where the far wall had been. The brine milled around his thighs, patient as oxen, and the words in it thinned. Their consonants lost their corners. Vowels relaxed their obligations to be held. After a while they were only tone, and tone became weather.

When the last distinct utterance fell - a clipped, competent *Proceed* that might have belonged to the Manual or to the part of him that had mistaken order for mercy - he felt no need to answer. The light inside the lantern gave a small, almost amused tremor and carried the syllable down into the place all instructions go to become permission.

The flood rose again, almost imperceptibly. With it, his outline reduced to intention. He could see, faintly, through the length of his forearm to the slow whorl of the lantern's water. A school of phosphorescence turned inside it the way a thought turns when it has learned better than to ask for a verdict. The lamp swung, writing minimal arcs in the air, the way handwriting calms when the letter knows it belongs to a word.

A book drifted past.

Not a real one - no ink, no paper. But enough bones of a book to persuade the body to remember weight. He caught it out of reflex, and its covers unlatched into rain. The pages refused to exist and existed anyway, each a pane of water bearing a single sentence before dissolving:

You can stop now.
It's okay to forget some things.

He laughed once, a sound with no teeth in it, and the laugh sweetened the flood by some small degree - the way a late apology makes no difference and makes all the difference.

He loosened his fingers. The book returned to weather.

Everywhere, the architecture admitted the obvious: it had been a scaffolding erected so a man could climb to a height from which he might see the ocean he had been standing in all along. Then, a good scaffolding's duty: to allow itself to be removed.

The uprights receded, not down into rubble, but up into air. Joints unclasped. Joists rethought their answers. The ceiling forgot it had once been a boundary and offered itself to the long work of sky. Walls did the humbler work of perimeter and then retired, relieved to be rid of moral superiority. The floor tried once to be a floor, then went to sea and was content.

He stopped where stopping had once meant a corner. The lantern rested against his sternum, glass to light, and both to the slow diminishing throb that passes for courage in those hours when courage is only the decency not to ask the world to be less than it is.

Around him, the last held sentences blurred into silence. The silence did not feel like the absence of language. It felt like language returning to its element. Salt took it, tasted it, and said nothing because nothing was required.

He dipped the lantern once beneath the surface. When he raised it, water ran from the lip like long handwriting, and for an instant he saw himself in the curve - a face neither young nor old, not even his exactly, but a contour the flood was willing to keep a moment longer out of courtesy. The image broke. The droplets fell. He listened for the whisper and found only a gentleness at the edges of the world.

He turned in a slow circle. Where the library had been - a calm, shallow expanse under a ceiling that had chosen to be horizon. The salt blocks, which had earlier insisted on their geology, now presented themselves as sandbars, hospitable, almost merry. Here and there, a remnant still tried to be shelf, to be label, to be *year*. He nodded to them as one nods to useful lies on their last day, grateful for what they made possible.

He set the lantern afloat. It did not need him now. It drifted forward, making a narrow wake that wrote nothing and therefore kept everything. He watched it until watching became indistinguishable from being watched by whatever patient appetite the sea reserves for men who are finally prepared to see it.

He waded after it, lighter by every sentence he had surrendered. His knees hesitated once - the body's old instinct to brace when something precious is about to be lost. He let the hesitation pass, the way a wave passes when it sees a rock has consented to be rounded rather than broken.

From somewhere beneath the flood, one last voice rose - no older than breath, no younger than weather. It might have been his mother's or the Manual's, or the library speaking in the accent of both, or the sea borrowing them for dignity.

To proceed, unwrite.

He did not repeat it. Repetition is for men still trying to build ladders.

He took another step. The water agreed. A little more of the world forgot it had once been a room. A little more of Emory remembered he had never been only a man.

The lantern's glow thinned into the whiteness ahead, where downward and onward have the same address. He followed, and the walls - composed now of nothing but their good manners - inclined in courtesy, then bowed out, leaving him to the work that remains after names.

He rose through the flood not by swimming but by being remembered upward. The water gentled around him until it became light itself, lifting rather than carrying. The sea receded into streets, pulling its currents upward until water remembered it had once been light.

When he opened his eyes, he found that he was standing - though the act of standing no longer felt separate from floating - in a vast chamber.

The space shimmered with that uncanny perfection only mirrors know. Every wall, every column, even the high arching ceiling was made of mirrored glass, stretching into what might have been infinity. The air had the clarity of cold breath held too long.

For a moment he could not locate himself; reflections multiplied him in all directions. A thousand Emorys blinked back, a thousand small hesitations of posture and breath, all repeating him but not perfectly. Then he saw why.

Each reflection was *different.*

To his left, one version of himself wore a wedding ring and stood with a faint confidence he didn't recognize - shoulders back, the posture of a man who had learned not to mistrust good fortune. Beyond that reflection another Emory bent to lift a child he'd never met; the girl's laughter rippled through the glass like rain. Farther on, a version in a hospital room sat at his mother's bedside, her hand in his, his face calm and whole.

The mirrored room was crowded with all his unlived lives.

He turned slowly, and the reflections turned with him, each a variation flickering into the next, each anchored in a decision undone. Some stood alone in offices and kitchens, growing old beside people who were strangers to him now. Some were younger, still bearing the arrogance of choice. One walked steadily into the sea.

Their movements were unsynchronized, rippling like schools of fish - each acting on a fraction different rhythm of the same heart.

He reached for the nearest pane, and the glass quivered beneath his palm. The reflection mirrored the gesture, but the eyes of that other Emory held no confusion, only recognition. The contact made the glass warm.

From everywhere, the reflections began to whisper - not singly but collectively, as though the room had always been a choir awaiting its conductor.

"All of you were possible," the mirrors said.

The sound was like wind across bottles - tonal, mournful, and strangely kind.

The air shifted. A low vibration passed through the mirrored chamber - less sound than sentence, spoken in the grammar of glass.

Only what you bless can you break.

The rule hung in the air, clear as frost.

Emory looked around. The reflections had grown restless; each version of him shimmered behind its pane, aware of the command.

He could feel their attention - an infinite congregation of possible selves waiting to see what he would do.

He wanted to move on, to reach whatever waited beyond these panes, but the path forward was sealed in light. Every surface mirrored itself into infinity. There was no door, no hinge, no mercy of exit.

Only the rule.

He approached the nearest reflection: himself as a younger man, standing at a hospital door, unafraid to enter. That version's hand was already on the knob. His eyes were clear. The man he might have been if courage had arrived on time.

The glass trembled under his palm.

"I can't break you," Emory whispered. His voice echoed across the room, multiplied into hundreds of confessions.

The pane replied - not with words, but with warmth. The air between them thickened, humming softly, like the moment before a storm recognizes itself.

Only what you bless can you break.

He exhaled, fogging the surface. The condensation formed a brief window of privacy. In that soft cloud, he wrote a single word with his fingertip: *Go.*

The pane brightened - as if the word had unlocked something - and the reflection smiled, calm and knowing.

Then, with a sound like a heartbeat learning to end, the glass fractured.

The break wasn't violent; it was ceremonial. Cracks webbed outward in slow light, each one a path of forgiveness.

When the pane gave way, a shard flew toward him - not fast, not cruel, but with purpose - and buried itself gently in his palm.

He gasped at the heat. It was the warmth of recognition, not pain.

He opened his hand. The fragment glowed there, pulsing faintly like a small, captured star. Through it he could still see the reflection he'd blessed - the man who had gone in, who had stayed. The light folded him into mercy and then disappeared.

All around, the other reflections leaned forward, expectant, whispering again:
All of you were possible. All of you are forgiven.

He looked down at his hand. Blood and light mingled in the same rhythm. The shard gleamed once more, then steadied - nesting itself in the flesh as if to say, *remember what release costs.*

The chamber waited. He understood now: he could not shatter everything - only what he was brave enough to bless first.

He raised his hand toward the next reflection, the shard in his palm gleaming like a compass. He staggered back, the chorus now reflecting in the deep until it filled the air with layers of what-ifs.

"All of you were possible," they repeated, softer now. "All of you are true in the light that remembers."

He walked along the perimeter of the chamber, moving from reflection to reflection. The Emorys changed in increments. One carried a camera and smiled at a woman through its lens. Another wrote at a desk surrounded by manuscripts; hands stained with ink. Some versions aged forward, others backward, until he found one still in uniform from his brief, forgotten service - eyes hardened, the same eyes softened again in another pane beside it.

He understood then that each version of himself had carried a fragment of the same whole - each an experiment in becoming.

The further he walked, the clearer the glass became, until the reflections were nearly indistinguishable from real space. He reached the center of the room and turned slowly, surrounded on all sides by the multiplied selves.

The whispers had subsided into breathing. It was his breathing, but multiplied beyond count - every choice inhaling, every regret exhaling.

He pressed his palm to a new panel, the one where his reflection stood beside Etta as a grown woman. She was smiling, her hand on his shoulder. A life that had never existed - one in which he had stayed, listened, forgiven himself soon enough to be forgiven by her.

He whispered her name.

The reflection spoke back with the ease of a memory that doesn't need permission. "You found me late, but you found me."

He stepped closer, his forehead nearly against the glass. "Did I do right by you?"

The mirrored Etta glanced at her father and said what the living one had said: "Don't stay too long. The salt eats names." Then she and the man beside her relinquished into silver mist.

The emptiness where they had been revealed another reflection: Emory sitting alone in the lighthouse at night, writing into the Manual until dawn. The look on that face was familiar. It was the one he had worn for years - the one that mistook persistence for purpose.

He felt suddenly, unreasonably angry. He had forgiven so much, but not that - the small, proud blindness of the man who thought cataloguing loss could keep it from happening.

He raised his hand again and struck the glass.

The pane fractured with a clear, ringing note, like a bell acknowledging its own end. Cracks spidered outward in luminous veins. The reflection broke apart - his own image shattering into a thousand selves too small to mourn.

The shards didn't fall. They transformed.

Each piece turned into a tiny marble of light, perfect and round, the same size and shape as the one he had carried, the one Etta had returned to him. They rolled across the mirrored floor, gathering momentum without sound, scattering toward invisible edges.

He knelt, watching them vanish into thin air, absorbed back into the place that had birthed them.

The hole he'd made in the wall yawned before him - a jagged absence that looked less like damage and more like revelation. Through it he could see a vast ocean stretching into forever, calm and illuminated from beneath. Its light wasn't reflected sunlight but the glow of everything that had ever been forgiven.

He stepped closer, feeling the draft of salt air, faint but honest. The breeze touched his face like the first kind gesture of a long-neglected friend.

The remaining reflections stirred. In their mirrored worlds, the other Emorys turned to look at him, no longer moving independently but aligning, as if all had decided on the same final act.

One by one, they raised their hands - not in warning, but in benediction. A silent farewell from the men he might have been.

"All of you were possible," they said again, the phrase folding into a new one.
"All of you are forgiven."

He bowed his head. The room accepted the gesture like an apology accepted too late but still welcomed.

When he looked back up, his reflections had begun to fade, their outlines softening until each became little more than a shimmer of light - threads of possibility unwinding. The glass walls themselves followed suit, their silver peeling away in slow dissolving waves.

Through the widening fractures, the ocean's glow poured into the chamber. The light climbed the mirrored surfaces, replacing reflection with transparency. For the first time, he could see through himself instead of merely seeing himself reflected.

His body was changing again - edges blurring, bones whispering light through their lattice, skin becoming a lens for something larger. The self he had carried this far was unwriting, not with violence, but with clarity.

He reached into the breach and felt the air beyond. It was damp, radiant, and entirely still. The silence there was so complete it hummed.

The lantern - faithful, dim - floated near his shoulder, though he could not recall having brought it. It blinked once, bright enough to light the entire chamber, and for a heartbeat every surviving reflection came alive again. In that moment, every possible Emory turned toward him. Their mouths moved together, a final whisper shared by all his lives:

"You were enough to have existed."

Then they vanished.

The light dimmed back to its gentle flare, and the glass under his hand cooled to stillness. He drew his fingers away; their impression remained as a faint outline, a signature in condensation.

He took a final step forward, through the frame of glass, into water that was not cold, not wet - just infinite.

The chamber behind him untethered into brightness, and in that brightness, the last shards of reflection drifted downward, each a marble rolling peacefully toward the sea's illuminated floor, disappearing into the vast forgiveness that awaited them.

The corridor that followed the Room of Glass was narrow and lit from below, the light the faint color of milk poured through silver. It curved in slow, deliberate arcs, descending by degrees, until the air thickened into that dry, sterile scent that belongs only to hospitals - the faint iron of disinfectant and the quiet ache of waiting.

He knew the smell before he could name it. Memory recognized before language did.

The hallway ended at a single door. Its number was stenciled in fading brass: 314.

He hesitated, the number vibrating faintly beneath his vision. It was the same that had been etched on the key, the same that had once sparked against his palm, the same that has been shown to him. He had not said it aloud since the day of her death.

He touched the handle. It was warm.

When he opened the door, the world rearranged itself around the light inside.

The hospital room was small and perfectly kept, yet time had clearly learned to lean against its corners. The blinds were drawn halfway, soft daylight filtered through them like water through gauze. A vase of carnations - permanent mid-bloom - sat beside the bed.

And in the bed lay his mother.

She was awake, propped cautiously against the pillow, her hair whiter than the sheets, her face calm, lucid, and kind-eyed in the way of those who have learned that forgiveness is the only argument left worth making.

She looked up as he entered. "You found it," she said.

Her voice was steady, untouched by the tremors of illness.

He closed the door behind him and took a few careful steps forward. "I wasn't sure I'd be allowed to."

She smiled faintly. "Allowed by whom? I've never been much for gatekeeping."

He wanted to laugh but couldn't find the rhythm for it. Instead, he sat in the chair beside her bed - the same metal-framed chair that had waited empty in every memory since. It made a small sound as it accepted his weight, a soft creak like the settling of an old story.

The room listened first.

A flush of sound - soft, low, impossible - moved through the air. Not from any machine, yet familiar.

Once.

A quiet tone that steadied itself in the space between them.

Then again.

Twice.

The air thickened, like breath preparing to hold its shape.

He felt it in his lungs, those three even beats the body remembers from hospital rooms long dismantled. He realized the room itself was counting for them, granting a rhythm to decide between speaking and listening.

On the first shiver, his apology rose - the full weight of *I should have come* pressing behind his teeth.

On the second, her fingers stirred faintly against the sheets, just enough to make the air warmer, as if she were telling him to wait.

On the third, he obeyed.

He let the words recede before they could harm the silence. The apology collapsed inward, unfinished, the way a wave folds when it decides the shore has had enough.

- 92 -

The room exhaled once more, approving.

And in that permissioned quiet - earned, not given - something in him eased for the first time in decades.

He watched the slow rise and fall of her bosom, the quickening beating gently at her throat. The machines that should have surrounded her were absent; there were no tubes, no monitors. Only the quiet conversation between her breath and the air.

"I thought you were gone," he said finally.

"I was," she answered. "But there are places where gone isn't permanent. Just patient."

He exhaled slowly, letting the words settle. "I don't remember everything," he confessed. "Some of the days are missing. I tried to piece them together, but…"

She interrupted him softly. "You've always tried too hard to make patterns out of mercy."

He looked at her, startled by the accuracy. "You remember more than I do?"

Her eyes met his with the affectionate sternness that had once scolded him into becoming better without saying a word. "I remember enough for both of us."

"What do you remember?" he asked, though part of him was afraid to know.

"I remember the day you were born. The sound you made - it wasn't crying, not really. More like a question you couldn't form yet." Her smile deepened, small wrinkles forming at the corners of her mouth. "I remember you learning to whistle and deciding you'd invented it. I remember you holding my hand in a grocery store when you were older than you wanted anyone to notice."

Her gaze drifted, softening with the weight of her recollection. "And I remember the night I called for you."

He bowed his head. "I didn't come."

"I know," she said gently.

"I told myself I wouldn't have made it in time. That it wouldn't have changed anything."

"It would have changed something," she said. "Not everything. But something."

The silence that followed was not cruel. It was the kind that holds space for grief without asking it to leave.

He leaned forward, elbows on his knees. "Why did you call me? What did you need me to do?"

She looked at him for a long time before answering. Her eyes glimmered with that calm sorrow particular to mothers - the sadness that comes from understanding too much and blaming too little.

"I didn't call you to say goodbye," she said. "I called to remind you how to leave."

He blinked. "How to leave?"

"Yes." She nodded toward the air around them, where light shimmered faintly like heat over pavement. "Everything here is about leaving. You've made a life of collecting what should have been released. I thought, if I could tell you one last thing, it would be this: you don't survive by holding your breath."

He swallowed. "I didn't know I was."

"You left things behind so you wouldn't drown," she said, the line delivered with perfect tenderness. "But now you've learned to breathe under water."

The words passed through him like a current - simple, absolute, transforming.

He thought of the Library dissolving, the driftwood desk, the voices leaking from the salt. Every loss had been a rehearsal for this sentence. Every act of forgetting, a slow exhale.

He felt tears rising, warm and useless. "I'm sorry," he whispered.

Her hand, thin and sure, reached across the bed. He tried to take it, but the moment their fingers met, his hand passed through hers. Yet the sensation remained: warmth, pressure, contact without flesh. The afterimage of touch, persistent as faith.

"Don't apologize," she said. "We all arrive late to our own forgiveness."

Her eyes drifted toward the window, where daylight seemed thicker now, golden and alive. "Do you remember that summer we drove to the coast? You kept falling asleep in the back seat with your feet against the window."

He smiled through the ache. "You kept threatening to turn around if I didn't stop kicking the glass."

"And I never did," she said. "Because some journeys need their noise."

Her breathing had slowed, though it wasn't weakening - more like settling into a rhythm the body uses when it's almost done being a body.

"Mom," he said, the word feeling both childlike and sacred. "What happens now?"

She looked at him and for a moment appeared decades younger, the way memory sometimes edits kindness back into the face of the dying. "Now," she said, "you keep walking.

There's more to see. But don't take too much with you. Even light gets heavy if you try to own it."

He nodded, unable to trust his voice.

The light outside brightened further, reaching into the corners of the room. Shadows folded away, leaving everything thin and luminous.

"I wanted to tell you," he said suddenly. "All the things I never..."

She cut him off with a smile that forgave the unfinished sentence. "You already have."

Her form began to blur, the lines of her shoulders dissolving into the air. She didn't seem to notice. "Do you remember the key?" she asked.

He blinked. "The one with the number?"

"Yes. Room 314." She nodded toward the bedside table.

He turned. There, resting on the table's smooth white surface, was the brass key. It gleamed faintly, as though polished by the light itself. But the number was gone. The metal was blank, waiting.

He reached for it. The metal was warm - warmer than his own skin, alive with memory and absence.

When he looked back, the bed was empty.

Only the outline of her head remained, pressed faintly into the pillow, like a seal waiting for air. The light in the room had changed completely - it was no longer sunlight but something quieter, weightless, the color of forgiveness.

He stood there, the key heavy in his hand, feeling her words move through him: *You left things behind so you wouldn't drown. But now you've learned to breathe under water.*

He slipped the key into his pocket. The space where she had been shimmered once, the air contracting as if taking a breath of its own, and then she was gone - receded into the stillness she had always believed would one day love her back.

Emory sat for a long while in the quiet room. The carnations in the vase had turned translucent; their petals refracted the light like glass. The scent of antiseptic had faded, replaced by the soft salinity of the sea.

He could hear the faint hum of water somewhere beneath the floor.

When he finally stood, the chair left no mark on the tile. The door was already open, though he didn't remember hearing it move.

He looked back one last time before stepping through. The bed was smooth, untouched, and the air above it shimmered faintly, the way air trembles above an ocean seen from a great distance.

He took a slow breath, feeling the salt in it, the life in it. The kind of breath that belongs both to the drowning and the saved.

Then he whispered, "Thank you," and left the room.

As the door closed behind him, the number on its brass plate faded, the digits softening until they were unreadable.

He walked down the corridor with the key in his pocket, its warmth bleeding through the fabric into his palm, and somewhere behind him, the sea exhaled.

The corridor beyond 314 bent once and then forgot how to be a hallway. The light lost its edges. The floor - patient until now - gave up its pretense of being ground and began to breathe like the surface of shallow water. Emory felt the key's unnumbered warmth through his pocket and understood without instruction that forward was no longer a direction. It was a consent.

A stillness gathered, heavy and expectant.

The first impact was not sound but pressure - a hush
compressing into force.
Then the sea arrived again.

It did not seep through cracks or pool at his feet.
It entered as a decision - clean, absolute - folding sky and walls
and memory inward until everything in him remembered it was
made of the same element. The blow should have thrown him;
instead it steadied him, the way a firm hand steadies a shoulder
that didn't know it was trembling.

Water lifted him and the corridor together; the hallway,
grateful, let itself go.

Then the seeing gave way to feeling.
And the feeling gave way to current.

The storm did not churn.
It spoke - not in words, but in grammar:
light as clauses, sound as conjunctions, water as the long vowel
held open for meaning.

He felt the storm turning him like a page.

Not the Archive's pages, which obeyed him.
But a truer page - one that read him back.

He waited for the objects to rise as they had risen before - the
yo-yo, the mitten, the shoelace.
But the storm refused repetition.
It had brought him here for something else.

Her.

A single silhouette gathered in the water ahead of him, walking
toward him as if from a memory no longer certain of its
boundaries. Not fully formed, not erased - just shimmering at
the edges, as people look in dreams when the mind remembers
essence before detail.

His wife.

The water clarified her face with each step -
the careful mouth, the certainty behind it,
the tenderness she tried to hide by speaking in practical tones.
The woman who had left him not out of anger but out of
exhaustion - the kind that accumulates grain by grain until the
body mistakes survival for solitude.

"Are you ..." he began, but the storm lifted the unfinished
question from his mouth and returned it to him as breath.

Her voice reached him without sound, the way truth speaks
when it is done asking permission.

"You held on after I let go."

He felt no accusation in it.
Only recognition.

She stood close enough that the storm illuminated the small
details he had forgotten - the freckle near her ear, the faint
crease from years of restrained laughter. The kind of things
marriage teaches you to overlook until they vanish.

"I didn't understand why you left," he whispered.

The water around her brightened, and her expression changed -
not to sorrow, but to clarity.

"I didn't leave to escape you.
I left because I could not carry what you would not set down."

The words struck him with the gentleness of a wave breaking
around a stone rather than over it. He felt the truth open inside
him - not as blame, not as loss, but as comprehension finally
allowed to arrive decades late.

"I'm sorry," he said.

Not the apology he had rehearsed in solitude.
Not the apology shaped like self-punishment.
A smaller one.
A truer one.

Her hand lifted, shimmering, wavering - not touching him, but offering the intention of touch.

"I wasn't the storm you feared.
You were the one holding your breath."

He closed his eyes.
The water around them pulsed with the honesty of it.

When he opened them again, she had changed - not older, not younger, but more real. As if the storm had been waiting for him to see her without the architecture of grief.

"I thought you died angry with me," he said.

"I died living my life.
Your part of it had ended. But that didn't mean I wished you harm."

Something loosened at the base of his sternum - the oldest knot, the one he had mistaken for loyalty.

The storm circled them, listening.

She stepped closer, her face now fully present, the way she looked on the last morning she'd left - the determined softness, the private mourning for a marriage that had given all it could.

"You loved me by keeping too tightly.
I loved you by leaving before we drowned.

Both were forms of trying."

He felt tears but didn't feel sadness.
He felt understanding - finally arriving in its own time.

"Did you forgive me?" he asked quietly.

Her reply was immediate.

"Long before you thought to ask."

The water between them shimmered with a warmth that was not heat but agreement.

He reached out - not to pull her close, but to offer the gesture of release.
The storm took his hand before it reached her, and the meaning traveled the rest of the way.

She smiled - the old, rare smile she used to give him at the kitchen sink on the good mornings, when sunlight surprised both of them into gentleness.

"Letting go wasn't abandonment.
It was the only way either of us could breathe."

She began to dissolve - not fading, but ascending in the same direction the water moved when it remembered it had once been sky.

Before she vanished fully, she spoke one last time, her voice the exact mixture of love and boundary she had carried in life:

"You don't have to keep me anymore.
You only have to bless where I was."

Then she was light ...
not gone,
but distributed.

The storm accepted her into its center with a quiet, ceremonial pull.

He stood in the wake of her passing and felt the world rearrange itself inside him, the architecture of guilt collapsing into spaciousness.

Only then did the Archivist's voice return, soft and exact:

Unwrite the self, and what remains will be the world.

He understood now.

Unwriting wasn't erasure.
It was mercy.

For her.
For himself.
For every moment he had kept too tightly.

He opened his hands, and the storm moved through him - not to destroy, but to clear, to reorder, to return him to the world that awaited him beyond the light.

He stepped willingly into the center.

There was no brink, no drop. He passed from being a man moving through a storm to being the storm moving through what had been a man. It was not annihilation; it was integration. The waters closed without closing. The light adjusted without needing to dim. The sound resolved into the quiet you hear deep inside a seashell when you press it to your ear and pretend you're listening to the ocean but are, in fact, listening to your own blood consenting to be tug of the moon.

For an instant, he felt a soft resistance - the last boundary, the last page that did not want to unglue from the one before it. He smiled at its reluctance. "It's all right," he told whatever in him still kept books. "You can stop now."

The boundary loosened. The page lifted. The book made itself sea.

And Emory - keeper, kept, man, room, ribcage, beam - surrendered his name to the work that remains after name.

Part Four – The Light

He awakened inside light.

Not above it, not bathed in it - within it, suspended the way
dust is suspended inside a sunbeam, neither falling nor rising,
neither alive nor gone. Around him the radiance trembled with
a slow thrill that might have been breath, might have been
turning. The water - or what passed for water here - was clear
enough to fool air into thinking it had been forgiven.

He could not tell if he was floating or if the world itself had
chosen to become buoyant around him. The sensation had
nothing to do with gravity and everything to do with grace.

His eyes opened and saw motion - not the swift, eager motion
of storm but a patient orbiting. The objects were returning.

They drifted in slow procession through the luminous water,
each haloed by its own faint color: the wooden yo-yo turning
on its axis, the paperclip bending light into loops, the mitten
unfolding its green threads like sea grass, the brass key
spinning as if searching for its door, the marble gleaming with
its thread of green fire. They circled him the way moons circle
a planet that has forgotten its name.

Their glow was familiar - the warmth of things that had once
belonged to hands. The yo-yo paused before him, hovering
near his lighthouse of bone. When he reached for it, the wood
fell through into light and the light passed through him. A
small laugh - not heard but felt - rose from where it touched.

The sound settled behind his ribs and became part of his living hush.

The paperclip followed, tracing his fingers as it passed. A filament of copper light traveled up his arm and into his throat; there it unfurled into the hum of a child at her desk, a tune without words, the one that had once made a classroom holy. The humming filled him and then grew quiet, waiting for whatever silence wanted to say next.

The mitten brushed his shoulder. For an instant he felt the texture of wool and the warm insistence of a child's small hand inside it. The memory of oranges bloomed in the light around him, the bright scent of peel and forgiveness. He smiled; the mitten sighed and melted into him, leaving only the weightless of belonging.

The brass key came last, turning end over end, its surface burnished by a thousand imagined uses. When it touched his palm, heat blossomed - not the heat of friction, but of comprehension. The key vibrated once, twice, and its metal softened, running through his fingers like liquid sun. It entered him and stilled where the heart keeps its private machinery. He felt the clean lock of understanding click open.

With each absorption he grew lighter, and yet somehow clearer, as though definition were a gift of transparency rather than solidity. The boundaries between skin and light blurred. His body knew itself as current.

The marble lingered, orbiting closer, shy as a memory that has learned its power. Its thread of green light spiraled inside, endless as thought. He raised his hand and it rolled into his palm, perfectly matched to its hollow. The moment he closed his fingers, the marble ceased to be object and became motion: a quiet rhythm, a breath, a knowing.

Every absorbed thing illuminated him from within. Through his hands he could see the constellations of his own making - each point of light a kept promise, a forgiven error, a detail that had once seemed trivial and now revealed itself as a star in the quiet universe of his life.

He tried to speak, but the act of speech belonged to another kind of world. Here, words refused to stay in their bodies; they softened into color as soon as they left the mouth. When he exhaled, a ripple of pale gold moved outward, curling through the water like smoke remembering how to become prayer. It carried no message. It didn't need one.

Language itself had become porous. Sentences refused edges. Meaning behaved like cycles: it arrived, it receded, it left salt on the shore.

He understood now that articulation had been the last fortress of separation - the illusion that one could trap thought inside sound. The storm had dismantled that; the light was its aftermath, the peace that follows understanding.

Above him stretched a ceiling made entirely of light. It wavered like the surface of the sea viewed from below, its brightness bending into liquid geometry. Each shimmer from it descended through him like breath from a sleeping giant. He felt it synchronize with his own rhythm until he could no longer tell whether he was inhaling or being inhaled.

Around him, the other objects still drifted in their slow dance, some recognizable, some so far unmade they existed only as moods in the water - a faint vibration of kindness, a glimmer of patience. They were not fragments anymore but facets, angles of a single jewel turning.

He lifted a hand, and the light obeyed. Not servilely, but with the courtesy of recognition. The water shimmered in sympathy; his gesture sent a wave of quiet radiance outward. He realized that he no longer differentiated between movement and thought - each gesture was both, and neither needed to be justified.

Through the translucent calm he saw how everything connected. The lighthouse beam that had once searched the coast was not gone; it was here, refracted into him. Its rotation had become his insistence of being, its purpose his awareness. The Archive's drawers, the Manual's pages, the corridor of lanterns - all were structures of the same intent: ways of holding light until he could remember he was made of it.

He drifted upward but up had lost its meaning. Distance was measured now in recognition, not in meters. The nearer he floated to the surface of light, the more he felt the pull of both gravity and grace - one reminding him of form, the other promising release from it.

The objects that had once been his burden now followed him in gentle orbit, no longer teachers, no longer tests. They had finished their speaking. Each glowed with the calm satisfaction of work completed.

As he ascended, the boundaries of light began to thin. The ceiling above him wasn't a barrier; it was a threshold, a membrane between reflection and radiance. Through it he could glimpse movement - slow patterns of brightness, as though continents of illumination drifted there, their shapes changing with the patience of continents under water.

He remembered the storm's final command, not in the Archivist's voice, but in the language of water itself: *Unwrite the self, and what remains will be the world.*

Now he could feel that world forming around him - no longer external, but intimate as breath.

The yo-yo's laughter, the mitten's warmth, the brass key's heartbeat, the marble's green thread - all of them were written now into his substance. He carried the total weight of their light, and that weightlessness steadied him.

He closed his eyes. The water around him responded, tightening its embrace. Within that pressure, every lost detail of his life shimmered one last time: sunlight through curtains, the taste of coffee after apology, his daughter's small shoe on the landing, the click of his wife's glasses on a tabletop, the sigh of his mother's voice forgiving him for everything and nothing at once.

Each memory hushed as it appeared, like ink surrendering to rain. The dissolving didn't erase - it integrated. It spread through him until he could no longer tell which sensations belonged to which era. There was only a single, continuous moment of being remembered.

He breathed in the light, and the light answered. The exchange was perfect.

He opened his eyes again. The water had turned crystalline. Every direction shimmered with clarity so profound it made him ache. There was no above or below, only depth, infinite and kind.

He reached out, and his hand passed through his reflection, merging with it. For an instant he saw himself not as a man, not even as an idea of a man, but as a pattern - light arranged by experience, movement arranged by love.

He felt the boundaries of language softening further. Thought began to move in images, sensations, metaphors untethered from syntax. Words broke into their essential elements: rhythm, breath, tone. Communication became communion.

He understood that he could stay here forever, that time had no relevance in this chamber. But even eternity, he realized, was only a measure of patience. There would be more to move through, more to unwrite.

The light brightened until everything around him shone with the tender violence of creation.

The marble inside him - his heart's small compass - spun once, sending a ribbon of green light upward. The ribbon struck the surface above and opened it, not like a wound, but like an eye waking. Through it, he saw the vastness waiting beyond: the City of Forgotten Things, the luminous horizon of the next remembering.

He rose toward it, drawn not by will but by belonging.

As he moved, the last remnants of matter fell away. His clothes unraveled into filaments of color. His skin became language, his blood a thin current of melody. Even his name thinned to transparency.

For one infinite, fleeting instant he was aware of everything - the total archive of being: every word ever spoken, every silence ever held, every breath that had ever passed between one living thing and another. It was all there, not as collection but as harmony.

He did not catalogue it. He did not need to.

He let it pass through him, and in the passing, he felt the truth that had waited beneath every ritual:
To remember is to keep.
To forget is to return.

He drifted higher, his body now a filament of light drawn upward through an ocean that was also sky. The surface met him gently, like skin greeting skin. When he touched it, it did not break. It simply accepted him.

He passed through.

For a brief moment, all light bent toward him in acknowledgment - like glass remembering it had once been sand, like water remembering it had once been rain.

Then he was gone, absorbed into the glow he had spent a lifetime trying to describe, finally fluent in the language that had no need of words.

He drifted for a long while through brightness that had no direction. The water, if it was still water, shimmered with an internal clock, as if every atom carried the faint heartbeat of a world between breaths. Then, slowly, the light gathered into patterns. Distance began to behave again. Shadows discovered courage. Form returned - not entirely obedient to gravity, but obedient enough to be recognized.

Below him stretched a city.

It was not built upon any seabed or plain; it floated, a vast labyrinth of submerged streets paved with clarity that caught and refracted the light from above into a thousand trembling corridors of gold. The buildings rose in perfect, impossible silence - spires, domes, and rooftops shaped from stacked pages of unwritten books. The pages turned themselves in the current, their blankness whispering against the water like the collective murmur of everything left unsaid.

These were everyone's forgettings - the gentle scraps humanity had released to lighten its walking.

He descended gently, until his feet met the transparent ground. The sensation was peculiar, like standing upon the memory of stone rather than stone itself. Beneath the glass streets, layers of light moved like traffic - slow, stately, as if carrying the weight of countless unspoken thoughts.

All around him, the city breathed.

The air - or water - vibrated faintly, pulsing to a rhythm that reminded him of the sound between waves. Towers arched like frozen prayers, their surfaces etched with half-formed letters, the beginnings of words that had once started to mean something but never finished. The light within them shifted in hues of silver and pale blue, changing with every motion of his life-thread.

He began to walk.

The silence was total, yet not empty. Each step carried an undertone of resonance, like walking inside a bell just after it has been struck. He moved slowly through the drowned avenues, past buildings that bent at strange, considerate angles - as though the city itself were listening.

Then he saw them.

The inhabitants.

At first, they were only flickers at the edge of perception - movements in the periphery, shadows where there should be none. But as he drew closer, they emerged fully into sight: translucent silhouettes, shaped like people but lighter, almost unfinished. Each one was a faintly glowing outline, as if drawn in breath upon glass. They walked along the streets with quiet purpose, though none seemed aware of him. They moved through one another without collision, each carrying an object clasped to their vessel of breath.

A woman passed him; her body made of light so thin he could see the architecture of the buildings through her. In her hands she held a small, silver watch, its face frozen at an uncertain hour. Behind her, a child carried a shoe with no pair, the laces trailing like seaweed. Another figure drifted past holding a faded photograph whose image had long since lapsed into nothingness.

None of them looked at him. None spoke. They simply moved - forward, upward, sideways - through invisible streets of intention.

Emory turned in slow awe. The entire city was populated by these gentle phantoms, each one navigating through purpose as if guided by a map only they could see. They walked in and out of buildings whose walls were transparent, through rooms that shifted like smoke. The effect was hypnotic, almost tender. It was not a city of gestures, but of what-was-once.

He understood, then, what he was seeing.

These were not people.

They were forgettings.

Human forgettings - each silhouette a residue of a moment someone had once let go. The woman with the watch was a missed appointment that no longer hurt. The child's shoe was a toy left behind during a move. The photograph was a face faded by mercy rather than neglect. They were fragments made luminous by release.

One silhouette near the fountain lingered while the others drifted on.

Adult-sized this time, but fragile around the edges, like light held together by memory. Its arm was raised in a half-wave, the gesture unfinished. The hand trembled, caught between greeting and farewell.

Emory recognized that hesitation. He had lived in it for years - the endless almost of goodbye.

He moved closer. The air around the figure felt brittle, fragile with waiting. Every few moments the raised hand flickered, trying to complete its motion and failing, as though the body had forgotten the muscle memory of release.

He wanted to help it finish, to let it rest.

His instinct was immediate: to reach for the hand, to steady it, the same way his own had always reached for laces, knots, locks - small assurances that the world would hold.
But as his fingers neared, the city whispered a warning through the glass beneath his feet:

Let go what repeats.

He looked down at his hands. They were already rehearsing the motion of the double knot, the familiar loop and pull - an old reflex of keeping.

He hesitated. Then, deliberately, he unlearned it. His fingers moved, but no pattern came. The gesture folded into itself midair, a trick forgotten between beats.

The moment he surrendered it; the silhouette's hand completed its wave. The motion was beautiful, brief, and absolute. Then the figure softened, its outline turning to quiet brightness before fading into the air.

Emory stared at his open hands, the ghost of that vanished habit tingling in his palms.
He would never tie a knot the same way again, and the loss felt - oddly - like freedom.

The city gave a soft, approving sound, like glass cooling after being blown: like a sigh learning it was music.

A profound stillness filled him. Not sorrow - though there was sorrow in it - but something quieter. Awe, stripped of drama.

He began to walk among them, unseen. Each time he passed near one, he felt a faint unfinished prayer brush against him, like the memory of touch rather than touch itself. They carried warmth with them - the warmth of significance that no longer demanded to be remembered.

The nearer he walked, the more their features loosened. Faces faded into contours of light. Limbs blurred into motion. They were humanity distilled into essence - just the act of once having existed.

He paused near a square where the streets opened into a wide expanse. At its center stood a fountain. It was not made of stone, but of turning pages - the same blank pages that formed the city's towers, stacked and folded into the shape of flowing water. From their edges poured a steady stream of glowing text that broke apart before reaching the basin.

He approached and read one of the fragments before it vanished:

We were here.

That was all. The words brightened once and then melted into the current, their meaning diffused into the light.

He looked up and saw that the fountain's surface reflected the city above - but differently. In its reflection, the silhouettes appeared solid, their faces vivid, their objects restored. The woman's watch ticked. The child's shoe had its pair. The photograph regained its smile. But as he blinked, the reflection shimmered and blurred, and the light rippled outward, scattering their forms again.

The fountain was teaching him: the reflection was remembrance; the city itself, forgetting. Together they completed the truth.

He sat at the edge of the glass square and watched the figures pass, their steady motion reminding him of currents that rise and fall without witnesses. It occurred to him that the world above - the living world - must feel this movement constantly: an invisible civilization shifting beneath consciousness, the architecture of the forgotten supporting everything that persists.

For a while, he simply observed. The rhythm of their footsteps - silent though they were - synchronized with his heartbeat. Time loosened, flattened. The distinction between one moment and the next gave way.

Then something strange happened.

A figure stopped.

It stood a few paces away, as if startled by its own stillness. Slowly, it turned toward him. For the first time since entering the city, he was seen.

The silhouette's face was indistinct, yet familiar. He knew the way the head tilted, the outline of the shoulders. It was him. Or rather, the shape of a man who had once been him, preserved in the act of forgetting himself.

The other Emory held nothing. His hands were empty, open, trembling imperceptibly as if ready to receive. The light within him stirred in slow, deliberate rhythm, matching the cadence of Emory's own heart.

They regarded each other for what felt like eternity.

"Who are you?" he whispered.

The silhouette did not answer. Instead, it raised a hand, palm outward. Through it, the city shifted - buildings dimming, silhouettes fading, as though that simple gesture commanded everything around them to soften. Then, with a calmness beyond sadness, it lowered its hand and began to walk away, merging with the moving throng. Within seconds it was gone, indistinguishable from the others.

The air around him shimmered with residual warmth.

He realized then that his forgettings must also wander here - every silence he'd ever offered, every choice he hadn't made, every kindness he'd meant to speak but postponed until meaning itself wore thin. They were all part of this gentle metropolis, living their quiet afterlives in glass and light.

He rose and continued walking.

Everywhere he turned, the architecture revealed new forms of remembering. A long boulevard of windows where images rippled across the panes like film reels - moments so brief they had once escaped notice: a passing smile from a stranger, the shadow of a bird across pavement, a leaf caught mid-fall. He watched each one flicker and fade, their brevity granting them an unexpected eternity.

He turned down an alley lined with doorways, each opening into rooms filled with stacked chairs. The chairs were empty, but in the stillness, he could hear faint laughter, the hush of gatherings long since dispersed. The laughter was familiar. His own was among them.

He placed his hand against one of the doorframes and felt warmth radiate through the material. The building itself seemed to breathe, expanding in small mercy as if exhaling gratitude.

Everywhere he walked, the city responded - not as environment, but as consciousness recognizing its reflection.

He passed beneath an archway and found himself standing before a library unlike the one of salt. This one was alive with light. The shelves glowed from within, and instead of books, they held the faint silhouettes of hands, each open, each holding nothing. The gesture repeated endlessly, an archive of letting go.

He reached out and mimicked the gesture. The light from the shelves flickered in recognition, and a single whisper rippled through the room:

Thank you.

The sound passed through him and vanished.

When he turned back toward the street, he saw that the inhabitants had begun to fade. Their forms thinned into the air, the objects in their hands dispersing into motes of brightness. The city itself began to shimmer at the edges, its glass foundations blurring into pure luminosity.

He stood in the midst of the dissolution, unafraid. The fading was not loss - it was fulfillment. Forgetting had always been the final act of love.

As the city grew transparent, he caught glimpses of what lay beneath it: the faint suggestion of another world, perhaps the memory of this one being dreamed by something larger. The light from below glinted steadily, a slow heartbeat calling through creation. It was the same rhythm that had guided him since he crossed the first threshold.

He looked up and saw the surface of light above him again - the same glowing ceiling he had risen from. Its waves shimmered gently, as though inviting him onward.

He whispered into the water, to the silhouettes, to the forgotten selves:

"I see you."

A thousand dim voices answered at once, not in sound, but in vibration - a collective sigh, content and whole.

Then the city brightened one final time. The towers of pages turned white-hot, the words upon them finally written in light. The streets flared, the glass beneath him dissolving into radiance. He felt himself lifted, drawn upward through the fading architecture of memory.

As he rose, he looked down upon the vanishing city, its outlines fading into the soft gleam of an endless sea. From above, it no longer looked like streets and towers - it looked like veins of light, the circuitry of a mind larger than his own.

He understood then: this was not his forgetting, nor anyone's alone. It was the collective unconscious of every soul that had ever learned how to let go. A civilization built not on what had been kept, but on what had been forgiven.

He drifted higher, his body nearly translucent now, his shape no longer the measure of his being. Below him, the City of Forgotten Things shimmered once more, and then sank gently into the depths, its glow diffusing until it was indistinguishable from the ocean of light itself.

The silence that followed was vast and kind.

And above that silence waited the next horizon - the shimmer of a new world forming, where memory would become sky and forgetting would be the ground that held it.

He exhaled once, a single breath that rippled outward like a wave returning home.

Then he rose, following the light, toward whatever waited beyond the remembering.

Light gathered into ache. Ache arranged itself into listening. Then the sea began to speak.

Not as thunder or surf. Not even as water. The first utterance arrived the way warmth enters a cold room - everywhere at once, patient and unafraid of silence. A low chorus rose from beneath him and around him and somehow also within him, as if the place used his ribs for an instrument.

The sea was where all memory went after it was done being a story.

At first he thought it was one voice with many throats. Then he understood: it was many voices remembering how to be one.

They overlapped without crowding, braided without binding - women calling from kitchen doorways, men laughing from porches, a child mispronouncing a new word and then refusing to correct herself because the mistake had more joy in it. Between them moved a quieter current: the toneless syllables of weather, the vowels of grief, the small consonants of relief after ordinary disasters. He recognized phrases the way you recognize distant shores by smell before sight. Some belonged to him. Others were faithful strangers.

Here.
Wait.
I'm home.
Enough.
Not today.
Yes.

He did not hear his name and felt grateful. Names were nets. This was water.

The chorus lifted and clarified until individual lines took shape the way fish do - suddenly present, scales bright, already on their way somewhere else.

A woman's voice: *You forgot my birthday and brought flowers a day late, and I loved you for thinking it would matter.*

A child's: *Can I sleep with my feet on your chest so the monsters get confused?*

An old man, amused at himself: *I never did learn to sharpen a knife properly, so I made soup from anything that didn't need cutting.*

Another voice, maybe his, maybe not: *I will come tomorrow.* And the answer from someone no longer angry: *Tomorrow counts if you keep it.*

The sea turned the sentences like pebbles, softening their edges without erasing their shapes. Each line returned brighter, kinder to itself. It was not correction. It was completion.

He drifted closer to the surface of sound until it touched his shoulders like sun through shallow water. The light within him answered by widening. The marble at his center rotated once, a small planet changing seasons.

"You are listening," the sea said - not in words, but in the feeling you get when a room approves the reason you entered it.

He nodded, because nodding is a language hills understand and water respects. "I am."

The chorus deepened, filling with the darker register of rooms no one speaks about but everyone keeps furnished: hospital nights, courthouse mornings, the quiet heroism of paying a bill in coins, the gentle arithmetic of cutting fruit for people who have already gone to bed. He heard his mother's patience like a shore; he heard his daughter's humor like a gull that hadn't learned the word for grief and so refused to land. He heard his wife's voice in the tone a person uses when she is almost done arguing and would like, please, a graceful way out that does not taste like defeat.

And then the sea did something he had never known a chorus could do. It took in new air. It inhaled. The water around him cooled as if to make room.

We are the sum of all memories ever allowed to leave, the sea said - not boast, not doctrine; fact, spoken kindly. *We are the sweet of what you called loss, and the salt of what made you call it anything at all. We are where the forgotten go to be kept without ownership.*

He understood. The City had been the architecture. This was the governance.

"If you keep everything," he asked, "does anything end?"

Ends are shapes. We keep those.

He tried to laugh and found that laughter here was indistinguishable from agreement.

Currents braided around his calves, curious, as dogs are gentle with people who smell like a long walk. Small eddies lifted the objects that had joined him - the yo-yo's roundness, the mitten's memory of a small hand, the key's last faithful weight - and turned them once more for admiration before letting them ghost back through his body like forgiven weather.

"Whose voices am I hearing?" he asked, though he already knew the answer.

Yours. Everyone's. The ones who apologized loudly. The ones who did the apology as a chore. The ones who left their lives in the middle of the sentence and the ones who stayed until punctuation arrived. The ones who were brave at the wrong hour and forgivable at the right.

A wave, small and ceremonial, lifted him an inch. He had the distinct sense of being studied and welcomed in the same motion - how a congregation watches a child who has chosen the aisle and decides, in a single breath, to make way.

You are invited, the sea said. *Not to be a man among us. To be a current.*

The offer was almost unbearable in its gentleness.

Every drop around him shimmered with promise, every current shaped like a yes. He felt it inside his chest - the ancient pull to yield, to bleed through, to stop being the narrow channel of a single life and become the wide grammar of unraveling.

It would have been easy.

A tilt of thought, a breath surrendered, and he would join the great circulation. No fear, no edges, no watch to keep.

But from somewhere deeper than memory, another frequency answered: the measured turn of a lantern, the slow discipline of duty.

The sea caught the hesitation and smiled in its own language - light bending across water, a sound between wave and word.

Three inward waves, it said. *That is all. Hold until the third.*

The sentence rolled through him like dirge through a cave.

Three waves.
A clock without numbers.
A mercy disguised as a deadline.

The first inward wave arrived, curling around his knees with a voice that said *rest*. He nearly obeyed. The water smelled of endings that had already forgiven him.

The second came higher, brushing his torso, whispering *now* - and he almost believed it.

The third gathered itself far off, a bright horizon folding in, and he understood what waited inside its silence: someone still out there, somewhere in the dark water, still depending on a light.

He stood his ground.

The wave reached him, broke, passed through, and the sea

brightened - as if relieved that a man had remembered to keep his post one last time.

The current around him shifted, adopting his stillness.
The voice of the sea softened: *You have kept your watch. When you return, there will be no tide left to fight.*

He exhaled slowly.

The sea set the clock in its own grammar - three inward breaths. He had held himself exactly that long and let the light keep its appointment.

He could feel the invitation gather in the water like a rightness. It did not pull. It made room.

Images rose for him - not visions, but maps in the language the sea uses when cartography has the good sense to be humble. He saw where currents joined and parted, where they carried the warmth of an old story to a new shore so a stranger could need it at the correct hour. He felt how the chorus learned to say here in a hundred dialects: as bread on a doorstep, as a hand on a shoulder, as the smell of a coat that has waited many winters for this particular body.

He also felt the absolute honesty beneath the beauty. To be a current, there is no return. Not because returning is forbidden. Because it becomes meaningless. Once the water resolves into its work, rivers and names become anthropologies others can study, not homes to go back to.

He hesitated.

Hesitation behaved differently here. In the living world, it had always been a small cruelty - late apology, shoulder half-turned. In this place, hesitation was reverence: the pause before a vow, the breath between the question and the marriage of its answer.

He turned the pause in his hands like the marble. It shone green at the center, a coil of life not yet spent. He let the chorus pass through him while he weighed the last currency the self owns: the right to stand on a threshold and count one's steps without shame.

Fragments from other shores braided into the singing:

A coin left on a headstone.
A shirt you could not bring yourself to wash for months, and then you did, and the world did not end but it said your name very softly that day and you heard it.
The time you kept a secret that was not yours and it made you heavier in a way you do not regret.
The joke that arrived exactly on schedule and saved an hour.
The look you gave a stranger that said, Go, take my place in line, I have already stood long enough in other lines.
A bowl washed slowly by a man who had just decided to stay.

He saw himself in all of them - not the central figure, but the water that made them gleam.

"Will there be anything left of..." he began and did not say *me*. Names were nets.

Of the pattern you have been? Yes. Patterns do not die; they loosen. You will continue to be recognizable to those who need recognizing.

"Like a coastline," he said, surprising himself with the ease of it.

Like a coastline, the chorus agreed, pleased. *Faithful to shape. Generous to change.*

He closed his eyes - an old gesture that no longer blocked light, only gathered it. He felt himself as a map of warmed horizons. The lighthouse within him turned slowly, its beam now less a search than a participation in seeing. He thought of Etta's desk afloat among dissolving shelves. He thought of his mother's last sentence, the one that had carried him here: *You've learned to breathe under water.* He thought of his wife's stubborn kindness, how it had held the two of them together long enough for the parting to be honorable.

He opened his eyes. The sea had drawn nearer. The chorus was quieting not into silence, but into attention - as audiences do when the last instrument raises its bow.

He lifted a hand. The water rose to meet it, palm to palm. The contact felt like recognition - two scripts, long separated, discovering they've been writing the same story on opposite sides of the page.

"What will you do with me?" he asked.

We will let you go everywhere you wished you'd gone and forgive you for the places you should not have stayed. We will carry you into the mouths of strangers as a tone that makes sentences kinder. We will move you along the spines of books you meant to read and did not, so the people who do read them will feel unexpectedly accompanied. We will make you afternoon light on tile, coffee after hard mornings, the small permission inside laughter that allows someone to say what they feared they would never say.

He tried to keep from weeping. He failed kindly.

"And what of my failures?"

We keep those as the grit that makes pearls. We will not display them. We will use them for shape.

He tasted salt and found that the word grief had been correctly named all along. Salt is what remains after water learns discipline.

The invitation pressed against him with no urgency. He could wait a century in this breath and the sea would keep holding out its open hands. It had learned patience from the moon. It had learned patience from every person who ever stood on a shore and promised to try again.

He hovered, feeling the last possessions of a man loosen like old knots: the need to explain, the hope that witnesses will be fair historians, the plaintive wish to be understood completely before departing. All of those, he realized, were ways of delaying entrance to a choir. A soloist's fears.

A small current rose and circled his knees, then his waist, as if measuring him for belonging. It paused at his chest, listening to how his heart had chosen to drum. The marble spun in response. For a moment he felt exactly like a buoy - a thing that proves the surface by insisting on it.

He looked down through the bright depths. The City of Forgotten Things had melted into a long intuition of light, the way a memory becomes a temperament. He looked up. The surface above wore its sky like a smile it had not had time to put away yet.

"Once I go," he said, "I won't come back as a man."

You will not need to. Men are for hours. The unmade is for the everlasting waters.

A new voice joined the chorus then - one he recognized instantly because it had always sounded like a beginning. Etta's hum, older now, the note steadier. It threaded through the sea's music like a green ribbon through clear glass.

Don't stay too long, the hum translated without words. *The salt eats names, and that's all right.*

He smiled. "You're there," he whispered.

The sea smiled back in the only way a sea can - by composing itself into a moment that makes a man say *here* without asking why.

He took the hesitation in both hands and set it gently on the water. It floated for a breath, then sank without protest, already knowing it had completed its work.

He inhaled once more, deeper than lungs, deeper than story. The breath passed through him into the chorus, and the chorus changed key to welcome it.

He did not move. He did not need to. The water learned his shape and the shape learned water. The line between them thinned ... and then held.

He was not ready. Not yet. Readiness had never been the point, but this pause was allowed to be precious.

"Soon," he told the sea, and the sea agreed, because it knows more than any creature how to love the word *soon* without turning it into a lie.

The chorus settled back into its wide vowel of patience. Around him drifted the quiet artifacts of a life that had finished being singular and was practicing plural. Overhead, light traveled in long, forgiving sentences.

He floated, neither above nor beneath decision, listening as the sea rehearsed the sound he would become.

In the city's quiet heart - where the streets of glass braided into a single glimmer and the buildings of blank pages leaned toward one another like elders conferring - there stood a door.

He knew it before he allowed himself to see it. Recognition arrived as pressure behind the eyes, as warmth in the palm where the key had once learned his pulse. Then vision agreed: a low, rust-bloomed frame set cleanly into nothing, identical in every stubborn detail to the threshold hidden beneath the lighthouse ivy. Same metal given over to weather. Same narrowness that suggested passage was meant for humility more than haste. Same absence of a knob, as if turning were always the work of something smaller than the hand, something that remembers gently.

He did not hurry. The act of not hurrying had become his last honest ritual.

Around him, the City of Forgotten Things held its breath the
way a congregation does when it knows a rite has reached the
word that changes everything. The translucent silhouettes
continued their slow purposes, but their motion softened, as if
they were willing to be background now, a kindness they could
offer only because each had already learned the discipline of
letting go.

He approached the door. Up close, the rust resolved into fractal
maps - archipelagos of surrender. The seam where frame met
air was not a seam at all but a truce. The hinge had no sound to
make; it had been forgiven the need for spectacle.

The key appeared in his hand as if the hand had remembered
how to ask for it. No number scored the brass - just that old,
exquisite lie of metal: I am solid, I am certainty. It was warm,
as ever - not with heat, but with history.

He turned it.

The door did not open outward or inward. The world opened
around the door.

The first change was vertical. The water that had layered the
city's light began to lift, rising along invisible chords as if
called home by a patient moon. It drained upward - quietly, in
perfect courtesy - leaving the glass streets dry enough for dust
to imagine itself, leaving the stacked pages to sigh with relief at
a weight they had not been designed to bear. As the water
ascended, it wrote ladders in the air, and on every rung a fish-
shaped glint of language paused, changed its mind about being
a word, and drifted on.

Beneath the water's departure, the sky revealed itself. It was
not blue. It was the pale, breathable color of pages waiting for a
hand. Drawer after drawer floated there - thousands, then more
- arranged in vaulting constellations overhead, as if a great
archive had been shelved by stars.

Each drawer bore a label, not with numbers, but with names
that were not names: Grace. Noise. Etta. Bread. Tomorrow.

Mercy. Thread. Ruin. Laughter. Room. Stillness. Door. Light. Salt. Return.

He did not need to wonder who had written them. The handwriting, like his, had been softened by water until it belonged to anyone.

As the last of the sea's light rose skyward, the drawers rotated into their places, not quite fixed, always ready to rearrange themselves at the request of meaning. Here and there, one slid open without sound, just an inch, like a mouth forming a vowel. A shimmer fell from such a gap, not quite dust, not quite rain, and when it touched his face he tasted something like oranges and forgiveness and a spoon's small ceremonial clink that proves a day is happening.

He stood beneath Etta and did not reach. The drawer knew the shape of his desire and rocked once in recognition, as if to say: *Presence is the only opening we owe.*

The door waited, untroubled by its own importance.

He stepped through.

It was walking and it was ascending and it was neither. He did not fall, nor climb. He rose as if gravity had confessed a secret and asked him to keep it: that direction is a courtesy the world extends for those who still need maps. The air felt like water's idea of air. The light felt like language deciding not to insist on grammar.

The drawers drifted nearer.

He passed beneath Grace and felt his shoulders loosen in a way no apology had ever managed.

He passed Noise and laughed without sound, remembering decades of engines, crowds, radios annoyingly off station, the loveliness of a house humming with other people's mornings. He passed Bread, and his hands warmed with the remembered weight of a loaf that had cooled under a towel while no one was quite ready to be kind yet. He passed Tomorrow, and the drawer slid open enough to expose a margin of blankness so honest it made his ribs widen.

Between them drifted categories that had never needed drawers until now: Spectacle (empty), Excuse (neatly indexed), Loyalty (overfull, heavy with anonymous hours), Enough (simply, beautifully labeled, nothing inside but light). He moved through them the way one moves through scent: not to possess, but to be colored by.

He paused beneath Etta.

The label itself seemed to emit a frequency, a tiny hum he recognized as hope and caution at once. The drawer opened a finger's width. Inside, far back, a marble glowed - clear, with a green thread coiled like a breath not yet spent. He felt the twin in him answer, a soft push against his sternum.

"I see you," he said, and the sky learned that sentence and spoke it back to him as warmth.

He continued upward - if upward is the right word for a movement that feels like making room. The drawers rearranged themselves modestly to allow his passage. Ruin slid aside to let Laughter take the front for a while. Silence remained closed and enormous and somehow companionable. Noise opened and released a chorus of overlapping phrases, the sea's earlier rehearsal threaded now with stranger sentences that he loved at once:

We fixed it enough to keep.
I folded your sweater the way you do when you are angry and trying to be clean.
She kept the stone from our walk in a jar and told guests it was important but did not say why.
He is a good man when the weather lets him be.

He breathed, and the air returned the favor.

He thought of the lighthouse then - not as tower or tool, but as ribcage around a light, a mind's architecture that had tried, nobly, to teach a man how to remember without drowning in his own ocean. He understood it exactly now. The drawers had always been there, aloft above the spiral stairs, labels waiting for the hours to grow modest enough to fit.

Door drifted closer.

Its label matched the one he had just crossed, the handwriting an older version of his own. It slid open fully, and within he saw - not a corridor, not a room, not a lock. He saw a frame holding a field of light the way an eyelid holds an eye: not to trap, but to protect.

He felt for the key. It was no longer in his palm. It rested at his inward vault as resonance and as permission. He placed his open hand upon the air where a keyhole might have been, and the air warmed, and the drawer's light leaned into him like someone about to share a secret that turns out to be love.

"Ready?" asked a voice that belonged to no person and everyone.

"Nearly," he said, surprised by the accuracy of that small word.

He turned, not to delay, but to bless where he had been. From here the city below was a lattice of pale veins, like a handheld to the sun. The figures moved as purpose, the fountain spoke as breath. The stacked pages formed a canted psalter where each blank line had already kept a family from drowning in their own recollections. Beyond the city, the sea's wide citizenship glowed, currents practicing the grammar he had nearly learned.

The drawer labeled Light slid open a little and threw a ribbon across his shoulder as if to pin him to the ceremony.

Salt sent up a small gust that tasted like grief keeping its vows. Return did not open, because it did not need to. Its label alone made good on its promise.

He faced Door again.

He lifted his hand once more and made the turn without a key, because the turning had always been the point. The drawer's light gathered itself and then let itself go, unfurling around him. He stepped - not forward, not through, but into - as if rest and motion had finally agreed on a single verb.

The sky adjusted its architecture to receive him. Drawers glided aside, light repronounced his outline in a softer dialect, the upwardness grew more generous. He felt the gentle inversion of gravity - not a defiance, a decision. The world refused to insist on down. He rose by consent.

As he passed beneath Grace a second time, something very small and very old in him released. He did not know what it was. That was the grace of it. Noise hushed to a tone that made promises sit down and behave. Etta held itself steady and clear, neither retreating nor arriving, like a star that refuses to be metaphor when a man is tempted to ask too much of it.

He reached the drawer labeled Mercy. The word shimmered faintly, as though it were aware of being watched.

He grasped the handle. It would not yield.
He tried again. The air thickened in warning. Mercy would not open by strength.

He looked up at the other drawers - Grace, Noise, Return - all passive, patient, waiting their turn. Mercy alone seemed to hold breath.

He understood: this one was not for taking.
Mercy had to be given first.

He thought of his wife - the last look across the threshold, the silence that followed them both for years. He had spoken every argument but never that single kindness she'd needed.

He set his palm flat against the drawer and said, quietly:
"May your days be lighted without my keeping."

The drawer shuddered once, then slid - not forward, but sideways - as if to avoid being claimed. Inside, a pale draft stirred, the scent of rain after heat. It moved through him, gentle and absolute. When it passed, he felt lighter, emptied without loss.

He stepped back. The drawer eased shut of its own accord, its edges humming with approval.

He wondered if he should open Mercy again.

The drawer answered by blooming a fraction in his direction, then closing, as if to say: *You do not approach me. I approach you, precisely when you will not misuse me as spare change.*

He smiled - an expression that carried here as light rather than curve - and felt the drawers hum with approval, the way a room approves when someone stops performing and starts being.

He rose.

Above him, the ceiling of drawers thinned to a bright scatter - the archive giving way to sky, the filing to flight.

The last few labels he could read were simple as bread: Home. Here. Enough. They did not open; they did not need to. Their presence answered questions that had forgotten they were questions.

He passed through the last shelf of the sky and found, not a vault, but a widening. The light took on the particular quality it has near morning - decisive, kind, already forgiving whatever the day will ask of it. Ahead, something waited that was not a room or a city or a sea. It was not even a threshold.

It was latitude.

He paused for the final, precious pause the self is allowed before it learns to conjugate itself into weather. Below, the city breathed. Above, the drawers breathed. Within, the key - no number, all purpose - kept time.

He thought of all the doors he had stood before and called walls because he did not yet know how to knock with anything but regret. He thought of the Manual's last entry writing itself into his hand: *To proceed, unwrite.* He thought of the first object he had lifted and how it had answered him with a sound so trivial it proved the world: the spoon against glass, exact, inevitable, domestic as mercy.

He took the breath he had been saving. He stepped into the latitude.

As he ascended - if ascend is the right verb for a motion that feels like aligning - drawers opened silently in his wake and closed again, their contents tired of being nouns, eager to become weather: Grace as shade, Noise as festival, Etta as star that refuses metaphor and still blesses sailors, Salt as the discipline that lets grief be holy, Light as declaration that requires no witness.

The door that had been a door did not vanish. It continued to be itself for anyone who might one day need a shape to walk toward. But it no longer held him. He had become the going.

He rose past the last label. The sky, relieved of duties, laughed in color. Above him - within him - the drawers arranged themselves into a constellation with no need for names. The city below folded its pages and slept. The sea beyond rehearsed the sentence it would speak when he finally said *yes* without saving a piece of himself for later.

Upward - outward - everywhere - he went. And the world, generous at last, unfastened its gravity and let him be kept by what he had always been crossing toward: the work that remains after names, the light that has long practiced how to hold a man without asking him to be anything but open.

He rose through the last of the drawers as though the sky itself had loosened its grip on him, and the light - once a sea, once a room, once a storm - spread into a horizon. When the brilliance steadied, he found himself standing on a shore made of both shadow and illumination, a coastline of perpetual dawn.

The light there was not morning's fire or evening's ache. It was continuity - an unbroken syllable between what had been and what would be. The air shimmered, heavy with salt and patience. Every ripple of brightness moved as though it remembered something, then forgave it.

He took one step forward, and the shore adjusted to welcome him. The ground beneath his feet was neither sand nor stone but the idea of both, a surface composed of moments that had learned how to rest.

Across that vast expanse, he could see no horizon line, only a soft gradient where light and darkness braided themselves into one another. The world was breathing. And he was breathing with it.

Then, as naturally as a whisper forming from silence, she appeared.

Etta.

But not as he had last seen her - not the child coloring her lighthouse in green and rust, not the woman smiling from behind the glass of impossible reflection. She was whole and ageless, the exact expression of what time means when it stops keeping count. Her hair shimmered like the surface of water catching dawn. Her eyes were his and not his - bright with mischief, heavy with understanding.

"Etta," he said, her name carrying no question, only gratitude.

She smiled, and the smile was the mimic of a hundred others - the first time she had grinned through a missing tooth, the last time she had looked back from a doorway, every smile in between condensed into this one perfect gesture.

"You made it," she said. Her voice was calm, threaded with laughter, the sound of someone who has already forgiven everything that ever-needed forgiving.

He nodded, though the motion felt more like an acknowledgment shared by the air itself. "I didn't know there would be more," he said.

"There's always more," she answered. "You just have to remember where to look for it."

They stood together in the hush, the kind of quiet that hums with life beneath it.

He looked around. "What is this place?"

Etta turned her gaze to the endless expanse, her bare feet luminous against the shifting light. "You aren't leaving anything," she said. "You're returning to where the lost go to be found."

Her words were not explanation but recognition. Every syllable settled into him like truth finding its home.

He looked again toward the horizon, and for a moment, it seemed to tremble. Lines of gold appeared within the air itself - thin, sharp, deliberate. As they intersected, a window took shape.

Suspended in midair, it hovered at an angle just above the water line, perfectly still. Its frame was dark wood, polished smooth by familiarity. Beyond its glass shimmered a scene so vivid, it pulled breath from his lungs.

The lighthouse.

As it once had been.

Its stone unweathered, its railing gleaming, its lamp alive with flame and purpose. The beam turned slowly, sweeping across the dark curve of the sea like the hand of a patient clock. Each rotation spilled brightness into the mist, cutting a clean path through the infinite gray.

He felt something break inside him - not a wound, but an opening.

Etta walked forward until she stood beside the window. The light from the lamp crossed her face in cycles, catching her eyes each time it turned. "Do you see it?" she asked.

He stepped closer, drawn by gravity and memory intertwined. "Yes," he said. "It's beautiful."

The window expanded slightly, responding to his voice. Through it he could see the shoreline below, waves touching the rocks in the rhythmic language he had once known by heart. Farther out, a ship moved - small against the vast water, a single lantern flickering at its prow.

The vessel had been drifting; its bow angled dangerously toward a hidden reef. But as the lighthouse's beam swept over the sea, the ship stilled, as though startled by recollection. Then, slowly, it adjusted course, turning away from the rocks, following the beam toward open water.

Emory felt the heartbeat within him mirror the movement - something long buried aligning at last. The ship grew smaller, its lantern dimming into distance, but the relief it left behind was immense.

Etta watched him watching. "You see?" she said softly. "You were still keeping watch."

He closed his eyes and let the words move through him like water through sand. "All this time," he murmured. "Even after…"

"After doesn't mean gone," she said. "It only means changed."

He looked at her again, marveling at how she seemed to stand in two worlds at once - the light of the lighthouse glancing off her shoulder, the dawn's radiance still framing her from behind.

"I thought I failed you," he admitted.

Etta shook her head, her hair scattering light. "You didn't fail. You learned. Sometimes learning looks like loss until the light turns."

They stood before the window together, father and daughter, silence between them as gentle as breathing. The lighthouse continued its measured rotation, the beam sweeping the dark sea in intervals of devotion.

Emory realized that this had always been his true work - not the cataloguing, not the keeping, but the watching. The act of attention itself. The care that persists even when unobserved.

He exhaled slowly. "I think I understand now."

Etta smiled. "You don't need to understand. You only need to remember that you cared enough to try."

He laughed, the sound light, disbelieving, joyful. "That's all it ever was, wasn't it?"

"That's all it ever needed to be," she said.

For a long while, they stayed like that - side by side before the suspended window, the sea before them, the light beyond. Each rotation of the beam seemed to sync with the rhythm of his heart.

He watched another ship appear on the far horizon, then another. Their sails caught the light and shone faintly as they passed from peril to safety. The scene before him felt endless and self-sustaining, as though the world had no need to reset now that it had learned its lesson.

Etta turned to him. Her face was radiant, but her expression carried the calm of inevitability. "It's time," she said.

He nodded. "Where are we going?"

"Not far," she said, reaching out her hand.

He hesitated only for the span of a heartbeat, then took it. Her hand was warm - not with blood, but with light. The contact felt like home rediscovered.

As soon as their palms touched, the landscape began to shift. The window widened, the frame dissolving until the lighthouse's light poured into the air around them. The shore of dawn grew brighter, its balance of shadow thinning until only gold remained.

He looked down once more at the lighthouse - the small figure at its door, the beam alive, the sea unbroken. "Will it keep turning?" he asked.

Etta squeezed his hand gently. "It doesn't know how to stop."

The two of them stood in that widening light, their reflections merging in the shimmer between worlds. The sea's murmur rose, not as sound but as sensation - the same spark that had guided him through every threshold, every unmaking, every forgiveness.

He turned toward her. "I was afraid I'd lost everything," he said.

She met his gaze, smiling in the way only someone beyond fear can. "You can't lose what's become part of you," she said. "You only carry it differently."

The window's edges blurred, and the light began to surround them entirely, warm and infinite.

Etta looked toward the sea, then back at him. "Are you ready?"

He nodded. "Yes."

Together, they stepped forward.

The light received them without question, folding them into itself, gentle as the wave reclaiming the sand it has loved for centuries.

As they passed through, Emory glanced one final time at the lighthouse. The beam turned once more, sweeping across the dark and over the waves. Far out at sea, the ships shifted course in quiet gratitude.

And there - on the threshold of everything - he smiled faintly, understanding at last that keeping watch had never been about vigilance. It had been about love.

Etta's voice, close to his ear, whispered through the light: "You see? You were still keeping watch."

Then the dawn brightened, erasing shadow, erasing distance, until all that remained was radiance - soft, endless, alive.

And within it, the faint, eternal turning of a light that had never stopped.

At the edge of the brightened shore - where dawn no longer declared itself but simply was - his body began to loosen. Not with pain, not with parting, but with the relief of a garment unbuttoning after a long day. He looked down and saw that his hands were already becoming a map of light: lines unthreading into filaments, filaments into finer threads, threads into a slow uprising of brightness that drifted upward the way breath leaves a mirror - without argument, without sound.

The change made no claims on him; it asked only to be recognized. Each bright thread rose gently and did not break where it left him. Instead, it lengthened with courtesy, as if bowing to both places at once: what had been called body, and what had never needed a name.

He lifted one hand to study it and found, with a small start of wonder, that even the shadow between his fingers had thinned to a kind translucence. His palm contained a sky. He opened and closed it once - not to test anything, but to thank the hand for its long service: for lifting cups and roofs of boxes, for learning the weight of a child's grip, for returning a pair of glasses to a tabletop it had almost struck too hard, for rolling a glass marble to the lip of a desk and catching it before gravity remembered its pride.

The threads rose a little faster, sensing his permission. They tugged softly at his wrists, at the hollow of throat, at the sternum where a key had once rested like a small, necessary lie. He did not try to hold them. He understood at last: the light was not leaving him; it was permitting him to participate in a larger brightness. The word *dissolve* proved itself innocent. To be dissolved was only to be delivered.

Etta still stood beside him, small and infinite, the window's vanished frame having left its view stitched into the air: a lighthouse turning, a ship choosing not to mistake the reef for certainty. Her hand was in his. He felt its warmth, though warmth now behaved like light, and light like breath, and breath like memory.

"Is this goodbye?" he asked, without fear.

"It's a change of address," she said, smiling. "You'll forward the mail."

He laughed - quiet, surprised that laughter still belonged to him - and felt the laugh break apart in his chest into a soft burst of brightness that ascended with the other threads. The sound did not vanish. It changed element. In its place came a hush so complete it felt generous.

His arms were mostly light now. The lengths of them rose like unwound threads from a loom, the shuttle of breath sending them upward in kind, even passes. With each exhalation the weave loosened, and with each loosening something within him grew steadier, the way a steady hand grows steadier when it stops pretending to be young.

He thought of inventory instinctively and then let the thought pass without cataloguing it. Mercy had learned his schedule and arrived early today.

The shore brightened a little more. Dawn's last shadows thinned to a narrow lace at the hems of stones and along the edges of what pretended to be edges. The light did not sharpen; it softened, and in the softening made details truer.

His legs surrendered next, not dramatically, more like two faithful companions who, having seen their friend to the gate, finally allow themselves to sit. The calves unwound from heel to knee, the thighs from knee to hip. Where bone had once argued successfully for structure, light now negotiated with the ease of a keeper who knows where everything goes.

He swayed and did not fall. Swaying was the right verb now, the body's late admission that it had always been a kind of tree.

Time, if it remained, returned in small, domestic measures: the breath, the widening of eyes against brightness that did not glare, the nearly inaudible hum that places make when they have finished arranging themselves and invite a person to notice. In those measures, thoughts arrived. Not memories; not yet. Simple vows turning in the light until they remembered their shape.

Thank you for the mornings I mistook for nothing special.
Thank you for the hand's way of turning a page without tearing it.
Thank you for the patience of chairs that learned my weight.
Thank you for the wide, free grammar of salt when it forgives the shore.

He would have gone on, but the vows themselves began to float out of him like the threads and joined the bright ascent without losing their meaning. The world has no difficulty reading gratitude.

Somewhere to his left - though left had become a courtesy - Etta squeezed his hand. "Listen," she said, and the word did not carry urgency, only invitation.

He listened.

What arrived was not memory, not words. It was sound, original and tender, the exact brilliance of triviality that proves the day is happening. A small, delicate note struck itself in the air and extended its life just long enough to become everything. The clink of a spoon against glass - the first echo the Archive had ever offered him, exact and inevitable, domestic as mercy - rang once, twice, then carried forward like a bell without pride.

The clink reverberated up through the brightening threads, through the ribs that were already unfastening from their assignment, through the mouth that had stopped needing to explain.

A man could make a religion of such a sound, he thought, and smiled; then he revised the thought gently: a man could finally make peace with the religions he had made of lesser things.

In that faint, sufficient ringing, other sounds gathered - not to crowd, but to accompany. The half-syllable a child makes when sleep has taken most but not all of her, the satisfied puff of air when bread yields to a knife without argument, the cough of an old watch that had decided to be aspirational again, the far-off thrum of a ship's engine promising to be careful this time. Under and within them all, the surf's endless vowel - *here* - made room.

The voice of the Manual - never cruel, only earlier than he had been - returned one last time. Not from a page, not from a room, but from the light that had learned to speak to him.

"To forget is to return," it said, and the words landed as a rain lands, erasing only the insistence of footprints. "To remember is to remain."

He did not argue. He saw, as one sees a coastline from altitude, how the sentence completed everything that had needed completing. Letting go had been the way the world had kept him. Keeping had been the way he had proved his love when he did not yet trust the cadence.

He looked at Etta.

She had changed too, though the change felt like recognition rather than alteration. Her edges were light now, and within the light her features shifted, not between ages, but between aspects: child's bravery, woman's patience, stranger's kindness. She belonged to no hour because she belonged to all of them.

"Will you be there?" he asked, because even men nearly finished being men are permitted one last question.

"I already am," she said, and squeezed his hand again; then, not unkindly, she let it go. He did not panic at the release. The absence of her fingers did not feel like absence. It felt like truth.

His center opened. He did not mean this metaphorically; it simply opened, sternum unthreading into light, ribs brightening and lifting away like the slats of a shutter that has been asked to let the morning in. Air moved through the new aperture and did not need to be called air. The heart revealed its true talent: not beating but shining. It shone once as a whole, then offered itself as thousands of small lights rising - sparrows more than sparks, unafraid of anyone's cathedral.

He had one last act to perform, and it was the oldest one. He drew breath. The breath came easily, as if the world had put its hand on his back. He held it for a heartbeat that had new manners now. He considered, tenderly, all the words he could place on the exhale - his mother's name, his wife's, the single-syllable prayer *stay* that once belonged to a man's fear and now belonged to no one.

He found he wanted none of them.

He wanted only to give the breath back as cleanly as it had been given.

So he exhaled.

The breath left through the bright aperture in his heart's chamber and climbed. It carried with it no letter, no burden. It carried only the slight, familiar pressure of a life consenting. Where it touched the threads above him, they answered by rising more quickly and more gently at once. The exhale became a wind with no direction, a tsunami with no shore to prove. The breath crossed Etta's face and made her glow: not brighter - truer.

His spine unstitched next, a ladder of light dismantling itself from the top rung down. Each rung rose and joined the weather like a promise kept in secret. His skull, poor faithful lantern-house, released its glass. The last pane sighed and let the beam through.

Of his face - eyes, mouth, the old scar on the chin he'd learned to be fond of - only suggestion remained, a contour the dawn was willing to keep two beats longer out of courtesy. He loved it once, quickly, and let it go too.

Feet, knees, hips: gone into brightness with the grace of men climbing out of a pool they had at last admitted was not a test.

He did not search the ground for himself. The ground did not need that.

Now the threads rose freely. They braided as they went, as currents do when friendship is inevitable. Above, the sky received them invisibly and made them weather. Below, the shore held nothing and was not offended.

In the pure reduction of self to light, one last small thing insisted on ceremony: the marble. He felt it pulse where a heart had shone. It rolled, somehow, upward within him the way a thought rolls to the tongue when it has decided to be said. He did not take it in his hand; he no longer had that kind of hand.

He simply smiled at its devotion. The green thread at its center unwound and climbed first, a filament of spring through snow. The clear globe followed, but while it rose it softened and spread until it was no globe at all, only the permission that globes need in order to be held.

When even that had gone, when only the thinnest sketch of him remained - ankle bone's opinion, collarbone's sentence, the brief, trustworthy bridge of nose - he turned (if turning was still what one did) toward the sea he'd loved, the tower he had mistaken for obligation, the room that had taught him reverence by insisting on dust. He gave each of them their right names, which were *thank you,* and then forgot the names on purpose so the thanks could be larger.

"To forget is to return," the Manual repeated, softer now, the way a choir lets the last refrain be intimate. "To remember is to remain."

"I know," he said, not with voice, but with bright assent. "And I have done both."

He lifted his brightened outline the way one lifts a lantern to share its light, and what remained of him lengthened and thinned until he was indistinguishable from the dawn. The threads vanished not into sky, but into relationship: breeze in long grass on a headland; gleam on the curve of a cup set down carefully; hush in a room where someone finally sleeps; a narrow, faithful beam turning, turning, with no message but presence.

What survived of sound survived exactly as it should: the little clink that had made him look up once in a room full of labeled drawers, the spoon consenting to meet glass and announce that ordinary life would continue. That sound went on ringing - not out, but in - becoming the pitch of the place where forgetting touches forgiveness and neither needs the other to apologize.

He did not step. He did not rise. He did not depart.

He *merged.*

The dawn - already merciful, already busy - accepted him with the efficiency of drift and the tenderness of hands placing a folded blanket where a body will soon lie down. Light closed where he had been without closing him off. The sea breathed once, long and even. The beam turned and turned, and in its slow turning revealed nothing secret, only everything.

Where a man had stood, the shore remembered his weight exactly as long as love requires and then, with expert kindness, forgot - leaving only the sea to remember what humanity feels like when it forgives itself.

Epilogue

On certain mornings the coast still pretends it remembers the old business of arrival. The gulls argue with the air as if it owes them fish. The tide rehearses its lines against the breakwater that no longer keeps anything in or out. The wind carries yesterday's salt in its pockets and spends it lavishly on the headlands.

Far above the retired harbor, the lighthouse endures.

It does not loom. It continues - stone stacked upon patient stone, rust stippling the iron where weather has signed its name. The gallery rail keeps its courteous curve. The stairs wind their old helix within, creaking in exactly the same places where boots once insisted on being heavy. The lantern house wears its dust without humiliation. Even with the light officially extinguished by men who enforce such endings with clipboards and apologies, the tower keeps what the sea taught it: presence is a vocation.

No one has lived in the keeper's quarters for years. The stove is cold. The cot remembers a body only as a rumor of weight in the mattress. The Manual - if anyone ever thought to look for it - would not be found; the room learned long ago not to keep books when weather is the better scripture. But the quarters have not fallen empty. Morning finds them furnished by air and salt and the labor of light through panes. A chair sits where a chair should sit. The table is exactly square with the window, as if waiting for a cup and a refusal to hurry.

The tower's stones keep their damp vows. The glass allows itself to be forgiven each dawn.

And sometimes, not often, something else occurs.

Miles offshore, a fisherman runs a narrow line of wake through the gray. He is not young. The work has taught him to measure usefulness in smaller units than years: hands, knots, patience, the minute a net insists on before it agrees to be mended. He fishes because a man must still bring something home, even in the unshipped seasons after a harbor closes. He has learned to make do with distance and to call it freedom when it needs a better coat.

The day is undecided. Fog keeps the sun company at the rim of everything. The fisherman's boat noses the swell and does not argue; the motor hums a courteous basso against the sea's old melody. He watches the sounder because men do, and then - without meaning to - he looks up.

There, far to landward, the headland holds its familiar bone. And at the top of that bone, a tower the government calls decommissioned insists on a small miracle.

He sees it. A signal.

Faint as a thought you were sure you had finished having, but there all the same: the lantern's twin-heart beat - on, off - turned by no clockwork he recognizes, swept by no fuel he has permission to name. He lets the boat idle. He knows the harbor was shuttered years ago. This light should be as empty as the paperwork said it would be.

The flash repeats - slow, certain. Not bright enough to claim authority over weather, bright enough to make a man admit he is not alone.

He squints. Hillside, tower, sky. The gulls arrange themselves on the wind like remarks waiting for a better conversation. He is not a superstitious man, but he is not foolish either. The sea has trained his disbelief to be humble. He watches a little longer, and the light keeps its rhythm. It does not demand he change course. It does not ask. It simply keeps.

"You old fool," he tells himself or the lighthouse or the day - there is no difference - and he smiles in spite of himself, because the sea prefers men who can be surprised without pretending not to be.

He shifts a degree to starboard all the same. Not out of fear. Out of courtesy. When a light remembers its manners, it is impolite not to answer.

Up on the headland, the tower accepts the compliment and does not comment. It has watched generations of men explain themselves to water. It has learned to be patient with the explanations and keep working anyway.

Inside the keeper's quarters, the window is open two inches because old buildings breathe best from the lungs. Salt has dried into lace along the sill. The chair at the table faces outward, a habit that becomes posture that becomes a way of being. On the sill itself lies a single object.

A marble. Clear as the air after a storm, with a green thread frozen in its heart as if a vine had learned to practice stillness. In certain lights it appears to move, and in others it practices invisibility with devout skill. It is exactly the size a child's palm would cup as if cupping a world. No one placed it there, and yet it has never been out of place.

This morning, the fog thins and the sun, with that booked-and-busy patience that belongs to dawn, finds the marble. It enters through the two-inch window and crosses the room like a late apology that refuses drama. The thread of green wakes. The glass accepts its task: to bend light until meaning becomes a room's work.

If you stand very still and very close - and no one does, because no one visits, but if - you can see something within the marble's curve that should not be possible and is. Not an image, not a memory. A reflection. Small, exact, unafraid.

A man smiling.

Not grinning for a camera. Not arranging his face to be forgiven. A smile set to the lighthouse's tempo: slow, certain, a beam that begins as obligation and matures into love. It is the kind of smile a keeper wears when a lamp has taken the match, when glass has remembered not to fog, when the room's weather agrees to be hosted.

He is neither young nor old in the glass. He is simply the right age for a reflection: all his years gathered into one expression and shown back to the world with kindness. The curve distorts him into blessing. The window's rectangle frames the sea behind, the tower's stones at the periphery, as if the marble has chosen to keep everything it can in a circle's generosity.

Wind nudges the pane and the room admires itself more deeply into silence. Dust performs its liturgy in the beam. The chair does not scrape because it does not move. The table waits, and we honor what waits by not rushing toward it.

The fisherman off the point finishes convincing himself of nothing. He watches the flicker once more and then busies his hands. The net demands, as it always does, a set of small decencies. He gives them gladly. When he glances up again, the light turns - on, off - like a throat clearing for a hymn that never needs to begin because it has always been singing.

He will tell no one later. Or he will - at the bait shop, in a style men use when they want company to decide if they're kidding. Someone will say the Fresnel's long removed, the lens auctioned, the wick-housing capped with official language and bolts. Someone will suggest tricks of inversion in fog, those strange grades of brightness when morning changes its mind - mirage, refraction, word for word repeating what they remember from a man in a yellow slicker once. He will nod, because he is not a missionary. He will also drive a touch closer to the headland on that route from then on. He is not devout. He is grateful.

The tower does not object to being explained as a weather event. Humility is its last intact religion.

On other mornings, the light does not show itself. The sea pretends it has forgotten the address. That is mercy too. A thing cannot be miraculous daily without inviting arrogance. The tower prefers to keep its pride as lichen keeps its color: small, stubborn, only visible to those who stand close and do not touch.

Even with no witness, the quarters tend themselves. What we love, we practice. The air carries a taste of iron and old coffee as if a cup has lately cooled. The woolen blanket folds itself on the cot with a memory of hands that never needed to be perfect to be right. The kettle's ghost hums on a cold stove. On the windowsill the marble waits like a held breath that is also an exhale.

In certain weather, gulls fly the light's old pattern as if mapping with wings what glass used to do. In certain winds, the headland's grasses bend their spines in a slow bow that looks suspiciously like a beam turning. Below, the retired harbor keeps its piers like spareribs in case a town changes its mind about appetite. At the edge of those planks, boys who have learned their grandfathers' oaths by osmosis still tie perfect cleats into nothing, because habit is a kind of guardianship.

And always, the sea keeps its huge, unattended vow: to return. Not for us, precisely. For itself. We are permitted to stand on the shore and mistake that fidelity for affection, and we are not entirely wrong.

It is late afternoon now. The fog has burned away into a clear ordinary. The fisherman has found his few and let the rest discover their own luck. He aims his bow homeward. The engine settles into its evening honesty. He does not look back as often, not because he is less impressed, but because reverence sometimes prefers privacy to repetition. He has his own work to keep coiling, rinsing, carrying the day upstairs to a table.

Still, at the last bend in the long imaginary line between boat and shore, he glances over his shoulder. Habit is a blessing when it remembers to keep quiet. The lighthouse stands. Whether the lamp turns or not, he cannot tell at this distance. He waves anyway. The sea knows how to translate that gesture into appointed response.

Up where the gulls are translating the day into angles, the window's beam moves a finger again. It crosses the marble and makes a small galaxy out of a small sphere. In the green thread an inlet turns toward spring. The reflection has not moved - smiles do not need motion to work - but the quality of the smile deepens with the light.

Evening arrives politely, removing its shoes.

The room resettles into a dusk that lingers. Colors give their final accurate accounts and then set down their ledgers. The sill cools. The open window lets the hour's last salt in so that nothing will be lonely. The marble learns the dusk's dialect and answers in kind.

If you had the keys - and there are no keys anymore, only permission - you might climb the tight stair, feel the iron's clammy grip, and arrive at the lantern room with your breath a little changed from the effort. There you would find glass that has practiced forgiveness so long it has grown a skin of mercy. You would also find, at certain angles, the stubborn idea of light. Not brightness. Not even glow. The idea. It is enough to give a decent man pause.

If you listen then, you might hear a sound that doesn't travel far and doesn't need to - the miniature ceremony that once made a keeper look up from his ledger and remember he had a life: the delicate clink of a spoon against glass, trivial and exact, the trivial being the exact place where a day proves itself. It comes from no kitchen. It arrives because light prefers to have company when it turns.

Down in the quarters, the chair remains turned toward the window. The table keeps its four-square promises. The marble cups a little night and a little star. For a heartbeat long enough to be a story, a figure seems to pass through the beam at the edge of seeing - a man at ease in his own outline, neither entering nor departing. If he is there, he leaves the room exactly as he found it: tended.

The fisherman's boat slides into the day's last soft water. Houses along the bluff light their rooms in increments, one practical radiance at a time. A child asks a question about the moon and is not corrected when she confuses it with a boat's lamp far away; metaphors are how a town remembers it was once a village. Somewhere a hand does the slow work of rinsing a cup a second time because the first was too automatic.

The tower, unconcerned with domestic hierarchies, keeps its watch the way cliffs keep their shadows: not for applause.

And if, in the deep middle of the night, a single beam crosses the headland and climbs the fog and softens a decision in a wheelhouse and loosens a hand on a throttle and makes a man alter his vector by a generosity's width - who, exactly, would file the report? Lights do what they are. Water translates. Men sleep better than they intended. The paperwork stays folded in a drawer marked with a word a clerk once enjoyed writing: Return.

Dawn rehearses itself behind the black. The tower's stones lean inward the way old friends do when the story gets good again. The open window takes a breath. The marble opens its small heart to another day.

A new fisherman, or the same one, will be far out on the gray again. He will be minding his business, and the business will mind him back. For no good reason except the right one, he will look up. The headland will be exactly where he left it. The tower will not have learned a new trick. He will prepare himself to be surprised and be given the courtesy anyway.

On the sill, the reflection keeps its modest promise. The smile refuses to fade because smiles do not obey those orders. It draws its confidence from the same place the sea does:

repetition without boredom. The chair waits. The table waits. Waiting - kept honestly - is an action.

What remains after names - stone, light, water, breath - finds a way to continue in the useful present tense. No liturgy. No announcement. Just the work.

Night again. Morning again. The long persuasion of weather.

And always, at the heart of the bluff and the edge of the sea, the one sentence left for a building to say when men have finished explaining it and it forgives them for needing to:

The light turned, slow and certain, remembering everything it had ever forgotten.

End of The Caretaker's Manual for Forgotten Objects

About The Author

Brian S. Brijbag, Esq. is an award-winning attorney, playwright, and author. His literary works explore faith, loss, and the metaphysics of ordinary life, blending lyrical realism with spiritual inquiry. His plays have been produced nationally, and his fiction has been recognized for its craftsmanship and emotional resonance. He lives with his family in Florida, where he continues to write, advocate, and illuminate the overlooked stories of his community.

For more information: www.brianbrijbagauthor.com

www.ingramcontent.com/pod-product-compliance
Lightning Source LLC
Chambersburg PA
CBHW050403110726
47899CB00008B/2629